THE LAST THING
I REMEMBER

ALSO BY ANDREW KLAVAN

The Long Way Home

The Truth of the Matter

(available November 2010)

THE LAST THING I REMEMBER

THE HOMELANDERS

BOOK ONE

by

ANDREW KLAVAN

THOMAS NELSON
Since 1798

NASHVILLE   DALLAS   MEXICO CITY   RIO DE JANEIRO

© 2009 by Andrew Klavan

All rights reserved. No portion of this book may be reproduced, stored in a retrieval system, or transmitted in any form or by any means—electronic, mechanical, photocopy, recording, scanning, or other—except for brief quotations in critical reviews or articles, without the prior written permission of the publisher.

Published in Nashville, Tennessee, by Thomas Nelson. Thomas Nelson is a registered trademark of Thomas Nelson, Inc.

Page design by Mandi Cofer.

Thomas Nelson, Inc. titles may be purchased in bulk for educational, business, fund-raising, or sales promotional use. For information, please e-mail SpecialMarkets@ThomasNelson.com.

Publisher's Note: This novel is a work of fiction. Names, characters, places, and incidents are either products of the author's imagination or used fictitiously. All characters are fictional, and any similarity to people living or dead is purely coincidental.

ISBN 978-1-59554-586-2 (TP)

Library of Congress Cataloging-in-Publication Data

Klavan, Andrew.
    The last thing I remember / by Andrew Klavan.
        p. cm. — (The Homelanders ; bk. 1)
    Summary: High school student Charlie West awakens bloody and bruised in a concrete bunker, only to discover that he has lost a year of his life and remembers nothing about escaping from prison after being convicted of murdering his former best friend, or why he is being pursued by both the law and a group of terrorists trying to bring down the government of the United States.
    ISBN 978-1-59554-607-4 (hardcover)
    [1. Amnesia—Fiction. 2. Terrorism—Fiction. 3. Fugitives from justice—Fiction. 4. Adventure and adventurers—Fiction.] I. Title.
    PZ7.K67823Las 2009
    [Fic]—dc22   2009001857

Printed in the United States of America

10 11 12 13 RRD 6 5 4 3 2 1

THIS BOOK IS FOR JACKSON KLAVAN

PART ONE

CHAPTER ONE

The Torture Room

Suddenly I woke up strapped to a chair.

"What . . . ?" I whispered.

Dazed, I looked around me. I was in a room with a concrete floor and cinder block walls. A single bare light-bulb hung glaring from a wire above me. Against the wall across from me was a set of white metal drawers. A tray was attached to it. There were instruments on the tray—awful instruments—blades and pincers and something that looked like a miniature version of those acetylene torches welders use. The instruments lay on a white cloth. The cloth was stained with blood.

The sight of the blood jolted me into full consciousness. I tried to move my arms and legs. I couldn't. That's when I saw the straps. One on each wrist holding me to the chair's metal arms. One on each ankle holding me to its metal legs. And there was blood here too. More blood. On the floor at my feet. On my white shirt, on my black slacks, on my arms. And there were bruises on my arms, dark purple bruises. And there were oozing burn marks on the backs of my hands.

I hurt. I kind of just realized it all at once. My whole body ached and stung inside and out. My shirt was soaking wet. My skin felt clammy with sweat. My mouth tasted like dirt. I smelled like garbage.

Have you ever had a nightmare, a really bad one, where you woke up and you could feel your heart hammering against the bed and you couldn't catch your breath? Then, as you started to understand that the nightmare wasn't real, that it was all a dream, your heart slowed down again and your breathing got deeper and you relaxed and thought, *Whew, that sure seemed real.*

Well, this was exactly the opposite. I opened my eyes expecting to see my bedroom at home, my black-belt certificate, my trophies, my poster of *The Lord of the Rings*. Instead, I was in what should have been a nightmare, but wasn't. It was real. And with every second, my heart beat harder. My breath came shorter. Panic flared up in me like a living flame.

Where was I? Where was my room? Where were my parents? What was happening to me? How did I get here?

Terrified, I racked my brain, trying to think, trying to figure it out, asking myself in the depths of my confusion and fear: what was the last thing I remembered . . . ?

CHAPTER TWO

An Ordinary Day

An ordinary day. That's it. An ordinary September day. That's all there was before the insanity began.

That night—that last night—I was in my room, working on my homework as usual. I had a history paper due. "What Is the Best Form of Government?" A classic Mr. Sherman assignment. Mr. Sherman liked to pretend he was some kind of radical. He wanted us to "question our assumptions" and "think outside the box." It never seemed to occur to him that sometimes the simple, most obvious answer might be the right one. "What Is the Best Form of

Government?" I wanted to title my paper, "Constitutional Democracy, You Doofus, What Do You Think?" But somehow I figured that might not be the best way to get a good grade.

So as ten o'clock rolled around, I was sitting at my computer, working on my arguments. About how people had the right to be free and choose their own leaders. About how leaders who thought they should be in charge no matter what, who thought they had all the answers or some super-duper system that was going to make things fair and perfect for everyone—people like kings and dictators and Communists—always wound up messing their countries up in the end, telling everyone what to say and do and murdering the people who didn't fit in with the way they wanted to run things.

It was hard work—and it didn't help that, at the same time I was polishing my deathless prose, I had Josh Lerner—GalaxyMaster, as he calls himself online—on the Instant Messenger. GalaxyMaster was watching an ancient episode of *Star Trek* on YouTube and sending me a message every time something cool or stupid happened. Which was, like, every two seconds. And which I could see for myself anyway because I had the same episode running on the upper right-hand corner of my computer, even though I'd turned the sound down low so I could listen to George Strait piping out of my iPod dock.

> GalaxyMaster: look at that rock! sooooo paper-machier!
>
> BBelt1: i know josh. im watching it.
>
> GalaxyMaster: Ooooo its so heavy. i cant lift it. roflmayo!
>
> BBelt1: josh I can c it.
>
> GalaxyMaster: that klingon mask is so fake!

GalaxyMaster could be kind of a dork sometimes. Plus he was making it tough for me to hold up my end of the conversation with Rick Donnelly, who was on my headset. I'd called him to tell him about the argument I'd had that evening with Alex Hauser, but then we'd gotten to talking about the history paper. Rick had Sherman for history too, and he was totally aware of Sherman's high level of doofy-os-itude. But Rick was the kind of guy who was always trying to play the angles, always trying to figure out what the teacher wanted to hear. His paper made the argument that Communism was theoretically the best form of government, but it just hadn't been done right yet.

"That's nuts," I told him. "They ought to have a sign outside those countries, like at McDonald's or something: 'Communism: Over 100 Million Murdered.'"

"Hey," said Rick. "All I know is that with Sherman, radicalism is where the *As* are. Follow the grades, my son. Follow the grades."

I laughed and shook my head and went on writing about the joys of liberty.

So that, basically, was me—just before ten on an ordinary Wednesday night in September. Writing my paper and IMing with Josh and talking with Rick and watching YouTube and listening to tunes on my iPod dock—and starting to fade out after a long, long day.

Then the clock in the living room downstairs chimed the hour. I could hear it through the floor. And about a nanosecond later, my mother—with a predictability that sometimes made me wonder if she were really some kind of automated device—called from the bottom of the stairs:

"Charlie. Ten o'clock. Time to get ready for bed."

I sighed. To my shame, I had the earliest school-night bedtime of any just-turned-seventeen-year-old I knew, and except in dire circumstances, it was nonnegotiable.

"Hey, I gotta shut down," I said to Rick.

"You're such a wuss."

"You're a Commie."

"If it'll get me into college."

"See you in the a.m." I clicked off and typed into my IM:

BBelt1: g2g.

GalaxyMaster: wuss.

BBelt1: nerd.

GalaxyMaster: cya.

BBelt1: bye!

Then I saved my paper into Sherman's online home-work file and shut down the computer.

Ten minutes later, I was lying in bed, paging through the latest issue of *Black Belt* magazine.

Five minutes after that, I laid the magazine on my bedside table. I reached up for the switch of the reading lamp set in the wall above me. My eyes went around the room one last time, from the computer to the tourna-ment trophies on my shelves to the black-belt certificate framed on my wall to the movie poster of *The Lord of the Rings*. Finally, I looked at the back of my hand. There was a number written on it in black marker. That made me smile to myself.

Then I snapped the light off. I said a quick goodnight prayer.

In sixty seconds, I was sound asleep.

CHAPTER THREE

"Kill Him"

Then, all at once, I woke up. There, in that bare, terrible room. Strapped to that chair. Hurt and helpless. With the awful instruments on the tray winking and glinting in the light from the single bare bulb dangling above.

How had it happened? Had I been kidnapped from my bed? Why? Who would've taken me? Who would want to hurt me? I was just a regular kid.

In my first panic, I struggled wildly, tying to break free of the straps. It was no good. They were made of some kind of canvas, strong. And the chair was bolted to the floor. I couldn't budge it. I thrashed and pulled, trying to rip myself out of the chair or to rip the chair out of the floor by main strength. Finally, I slumped, out of breath, exhausted.

The next moment, I heard voices. I tensed. I lifted my head, held still, listened. They were men's voices, murmuring, right outside the room, right outside the metal door.

My first instinct was to shout to them, to scream for help. But something stopped me. If I was here, someone had put me here. If I was hurt, someone had hurt me. Someone had strapped me in this chair. Someone had used those instruments on my flesh. The odds that the men outside that door were my friends seemed very slim.

So I kept my mouth shut. I listened to the low voices, straining with all my might to make out what they were saying over the pounding of my own pulse.

". . . Homelander One," said one voice.

A second voice said something I couldn't hear.

Then the first voice said, "We'll never get another shot at Yarrow."

When the second voice answered, I could only make out part of it: ". . . two more days . . . can send Orton . . . knows the bridge as well as West."

13

West. That was me. Charlie West. What were they talking about? What bridge? I didn't know about any bridge.

The flame of panic roared through me again. Without thinking, I renewed my struggles. Trying to pull my arms up, trying to wrestle my body free, trying to tilt the chair one way or the other. Useless, all of it.

Tears came into my eyes—tears of terror and frustration. This couldn't be happening. It didn't make any sense. Where were my mom and dad? Where was my life? Where was everything? It had to be a nightmare. It had to be.

Now there were footsteps in the hall outside. Someone new was approaching.

"Here's Waylon," the second voice said.

The footsteps stopped outside the door. The first voice spoke again—louder this time, clearer, more formal than before. It was the voice of a man speaking to his superior. It was easier for me to make out the words.

"Did you reach Prince?" the voice said.

The new voice answered—the voice of authority. Waylon. It sounded like an American name, but the voice had a thick foreign accent of some kind.

"I reached him. I told him everything."

"We did exactly what he said. Exactly what he told us," the first voice went on. I could hear his fear, his fear of what Prince might do to him if he failed.

"The kid may be telling the truth. You have to consider that," said the second voice. I could tell he was frightened too.

Waylon answered them with a voice that was ironic and smooth. He was enjoying their fear. I could hear it. "Don't worry. Prince understands. He doesn't hold you responsible. But whatever the truth is, the West boy is useless to us now."

I was straining so hard to hear that my body had gone rigid, my head leaning toward the door, my neck stretching out, my hands pulling hard against the straps.

But for another second or two, there was nothing. Only the silence and my trembling breath, my wildly beating heart.

Then in the same smooth, cool, ironic voice, Waylon said softly, "Kill him."

CHAPTER FOUR

The Word of the Day

I've heard that when you're about to die, your whole life flashes before your eyes in an instant. That's not what happened to me. I was too wild with panic, too crazy with confusion to remember my whole life. Instead, my brain was desperately trying to grab hold of something—of anything—anything that made some kind of sense, that offered some kind of explanation for this sudden madness, this pain and terror. But there was nothing, nothing that explained it, nothing I could hold on to. I felt as if I were slipping down a sheer wall of ice, slipping

16

down and down and down into emptiness, my fingers scrabbling for even the smallest handhold in the smooth, unbroken surface.

Eyes wide, body pulling wildly and uselessly against the straps, my mind raced back over that last day, the last day I remembered, hours flashing through my brain in a single second as I went back to before I had gone to bed that night, before I had finished writing my history paper, before the argument with Alex, back and back to the beginning of the morning . . .

The alarm clock had gone off at 7:00 a.m., a pounding bass and a wild guitar blasting out of the iPod dock. I reached out sleepily and felt for the off switch. Hit it and sank back into a half doze. Then, exactly ten minutes later by the digital numbers on the clock, my mother's voice reached me from the bottom of the stairs.

"Charlie! It's seven o'clock! Time to get ready for school!"

I groaned and rolled over, swinging my feet to the floor, sitting up on the edge of the mattress before I'd even opened my eyes. When I could, I stood up. I staggered out of my room and directly into the bathroom next door.

I assembled myself. Showered the bod. Brushed the teeth. Shaved the beard, which still sprouted only in patches on my cheeks, chin, and neck. Viewed the finished product in the mirror. Not bad. Tall enough—edging up toward six feet. Slim but with good shoulders, and a lot of muscle def from all my workouts. The face? I don't know. Presentable, I guess. Lean, serious, with a mop of brown hair spilling into it. Brown eyes. I'm good with the eyes. I try to keep them honest, you know. I try to make it so they're not afraid to look straight at anyone.

I went back to my room to get dressed. But before I started, I tore off the page of my desk calendar. It was a Word of the Day calendar, and I liked to read the new word and memorize it while I put my clothes on.

Today's word: *timorous*. "Timid, fearful, prone to be apprehensive."

Timorous. That was a good one. It was the perfect word to describe my mother.

Now don't get me wrong. Mom was a pretty good mom, all in all. There were a couple of times in my life when she even approached Mom Greatness. She was just . . . timorous. Timid, fearful. Prone to be apprehensive. As in frightened out of her wits about every little thing.

Are you feeling all right? You don't look good. Do you have a fever? Wash your hands after you touch that or you'll get sick. Don't walk on the road after six, the cars can't see you. Don't go into that section of town. Put on your jacket, you'll catch cold. On and on and on. When I rode my bike, she was afraid a car would hit me. When I drove the car, she was afraid I'd hit another car. Oh, and my karate— she hated that. If she'd had her way, I would have had to wear a full set of metal armor before going to practice. In fact, if she really had her way, I would've worn a full set of metal armor and then stayed home.

When I came down to breakfast that morning, she was turning a couple of fried eggs in a pan. As I walked to the kitchen table, passing about two full feet behind her, she said, "Careful, it's hot."

Dad was at the table already, reading the paper. The Word of the Day for Dad would have to be: *oblivious,* meaning "unmindful, unconscious, unaware." He wasn't always like that. Sometimes he could be pretty cool, pretty smart about things. But he was an engineer for a corporation that manufactured a lot of the secondary systems that go into airplanes—guidance and communication systems and things like that. And sometimes—times like now—when he was involved in some important project, his mind got occupied and it took a lot to get his attention. You basically had to win first prize at a karate tournament or get the Best Grade Point Average of the Year award or wreck the car or set the house on fire before he even realized you were there. Otherwise: oblivious. Unmindful, unconscious, unaware.

And finally: *overwrought* would have to be the Word of the Day for Amy, my older sister by one year. Overwrought—"extremely or excessively excited or agitated." Emo to the extremo, in other words. In fact, as I poured myself a glass of orange juice and sat down next to my dad, I could already hear her shouting from the door of her room down the hall: "Mo-om! I just don't have any others!" Whatever that meant. Something about clothes, probably. Whatever: the Amy crisis of the day. Overwrought.

"Ah, the cry of the wild older sister in her natural habitat," I muttered, rooting through the newspaper for the sports page.

"Hush," Mom said—but she laughed a little as she said it. She put a plate of eggs and toast in front of me and hurried off to deal with Amy before the poor child got so full of girlish anxiety that she exploded in a cloud of pink dust.

"So," murmured my dad's voice from somewhere behind his newspaper. "What've you got going on today?"

Even when he was in one of his oblivious phases, Dad seemed to feel it was his dadlike duty to ask me questions about my life from time to time. I'm not sure it was part of his duty to actually listen to the answers. Come to think of it, I'm not really sure he was actually behind the newspaper at all. I sometimes thought I could've ripped it away suddenly and found a mannequin sitting there with an MP3 player periodically spouting questions like "So—how's your schoolwork going?" and "So—how's the high school social scene shaping up?" The real Dad would have already been at his office.

Anyway, this time it was "So—what've you got going on today?" And I'm pretty sure I could've answered, "Today I unleash the first devastating attack in my long-planned war for world domination," and not gotten more than a "Hmm—that sounds interesting" from behind the paper.

I was about to try it when my jaw dropped open and my eyes went wide. I suddenly remembered something. I'd been so busy checking out my Word of the Day that I hadn't actually looked to see what day it was.

"Oh no," I said. "Is this Wednesday?"

"Hmm—that sounds interesting," said the Dad mannequin behind the paper.

I looked at the top of the newspaper. Yep, it was Wednesday, all right. Wednesday, September 15.

"Today's the day I give my karate demonstration!" I said. I had completely forgotten about it. The trouble was, I'd agreed to give the demonstration last June before school let out for the summer. The principal, Mr. Woodman, had asked if I'd do it, and I said sure, and he said save the date and I said okay—but I never wrote it down. I remembered it sometimes, and sometimes I forgot. Lately, I'd forgotten. I hadn't even been practicing for it.

I felt the first breath of airy nervousness in my chest, and my little heart went pitty-pat. It wasn't that I was unprepared. I practiced karate almost every day, and I was always ready to strut my stuff. And I knew I had a freshly washed *gi* and all the other materials I needed in my closet upstairs.

No, what made me nervous was that the demonstration was going to be given in first assembly. The entire eleventh grade would be watching. And the class officers—president, vice president, and treasurer—would be sitting, as always, in their official seats in the front row.

And the class vice president was Beth Summers. Who was so beautiful and so nice I can't even talk about it.

CHAPTER FIVE

My Right Leg

Karate. My karate demonstration. That's what flashed into my mind as I strained against the straps that held me to the chair. So the last day I remembered wasn't a completely ordinary day after all, was it? There was my karate demonstration with Beth Summers watching from the front row. Not that that explained anything. Not that it explained how I woke up scarred and burned and strapped to a chair with two men with orders to kill me about to walk through the door. But it did remind me of something. It forced a solid thought into my racing, panicking brain.

Karate. I was a black belt. I was a martial artist, a good one. I was trained to fight.

Now, okay, maybe you think that sounds funny. Maybe you think: how exactly was I going to fight when I was strapped to a chair that was bolted to the floor? How was I going to fight when all four of my weapons—both legs and both arms—were immobilized? How was I going to fight when the men ordered to kill me were right outside, were going to come through that door any second?

And I'll admit: it didn't look good. But as the thought of my martial arts training forced itself into my mind, another thought forced its way in as well. The Churchill Card.

My karate teacher—Sensei Mike—gave me the Churchill Card. He told me to fold it up and keep it in my wallet, and I always did and I always looked at it before I had to compete in a tournament or take an important test in school or do anything else where it came in handy. All it was was a 3 x 5 index card. Sensei Mike had written some words on it with a ballpoint pen. They were the words of Winston Churchill. Churchill was the prime minister of Great Britain during World

War II. When the Nazis had taken over most of Europe, when Hitler was trying to spread his evil, hateful, murderous philosophy all over the world, Churchill inspired the British to defend their little island. Hitler bombed them and bombed them, but, led by Churchill, the people endured and fought back and somehow held on until the United States came into the war to help them win.

This is what Churchill told them—this is what Sensei Mike had written on my card:

> Never give in, never give in, *never, never, never, never*—in nothing, great or small, large or petty—never give in except to convictions of honor and good sense. Never yield to force; never yield to the apparently overwhelming might of the enemy.

I didn't know how I'd gotten here. I didn't know how I had lain down one night in bed with a life full of school and homework and parents and friends and girls—and then awoken in this horrible room, in this searing pain, in this deadly danger. But I didn't have time to figure it out now. Somehow it had happened. Somehow I was here. For some reason, they were coming to kill me. And with me strapped down like this, there was no question that my enemies—whoever they were—had overwhelming might on their side.

If ever there was a moment to remember the words on the Churchill Card, this was it.

Never give in. Which, in this case, meant I had to look for a way out. I had to still the panic flaming through me, and think. *Think.* It did no good to pull and yank against the straps. They'd never break. It did no good to try to slip free of them. They were tight. It did no good to scream. If there were anyone around to help me, they'd've come by now.

I had to think—and look around—look for another way.

I looked. It wasn't easy. In my terror, I found it hard to get my eyes to keep still, to train them on things and take them in. I had to force myself to do it. I looked at my left wrist first. At the chair arm it was strapped to. Nothing. The strap was strong and secure. The metal of the chair was smooth. Same with my right wrist. My hand extended over the arm of the chair. I could open and close it into a fist. But there was nothing within reach, nothing I could get hold of.

What about my ankles? I had to lean forward in the chair as far as I could to get a look at the front of them, then lean over to the side to get another angle. On the left, it was the same as with my wrists. Nothing to see, nothing to use. A strap, a metal chair leg, a bolt holding the chair securely to the floor. Leaning forward to look at my right ankle, I saw more of the same. There was no way out.

My chest was getting tight. My stomach was turning sour. Tears of despair were blurring my vision.

Never give in, never, never, never, never.

I leaned over to the right to get the other angle on my strapped leg. And that's when I saw it.

It wasn't much. Just a rough spot in the chair leg. A little patch where the metal had maybe bumped into something, had somehow gotten scraped and damaged. The thing was, though, the rough spot was right above the strap on my ankle. And whatever had caused the damage had left a little ledge of metal sticking out above the scrape.

And it was sharp.

By lifting my foot, I could move the canvas strap on my right ankle against the sharp edge of the metal. I didn't have a lot of leeway, a lot of room to move. I couldn't actually cut through the canvas, but I might be able to wear a way through it if I had enough time.

28

I didn't. My time was up. Just then, the door opened, and the two men came into the room.

My heart would've sunk when I saw them, except my heart had already sunk so low there was nowhere left for it to go. But these two—these men—you could see it in their eyes: they were the worst kind of enemies to have. Not even evil—just obedient to evil, just dead in their hearts and minds and following blindly whatever orders they were given. Right now, their orders were "Kill him"— that meant me. One look at them, and I knew no matter what I said, they would follow those orders to the end.

They were dressed just like I was. White shirts, black slacks. The one on the left was white, slovenly, with limp black hair hanging over idiot eyes and a chunky belly pushing tight against his belt. The one on the right was smaller, thinner. Brown-skinned and foreign-looking with a narrow, jutting face like a rat's. He had a light in his dark eyes, a sort of breathless smile playing at the corner of his lips. He was excited, I could tell. He was looking forward to this. He liked hurting people. He liked watching them die.

The chunky thug closed the door behind him.

I looked at the two of them, too terrified to speak. I half expected them to just pull guns out and shoot me to death where I sat. They didn't, though, not right off. They came toward me. They stood over me.

And all the while, I kept lifting and lowering my foot. I couldn't look down—that would've given it away—so I couldn't be sure I was still rubbing the canvas strap against the sharp little irregularity in the metal of the chair leg. But I hoped I was. And I hoped they wouldn't notice. And I hoped the strap would start to tear. But I have to admit it: my hope wasn't very strong.

The chunky thug smiled stupidly. He talked stupidly, too, in a thick, dull voice. I got the feeling that *stupidly* was pretty much the way he did everything.

"Okay, you dumb punk, you asked for it," he said.

"That's right," said the rat-faced guy. His voice was light and breathless, excited like his eyes. He had an accent of some kind. "If you'd talked to us, maybe we could've helped you."

I kept lifting and lowering my foot. Hoping they wouldn't notice. Hoping the strap would tear. *Never give in.*

"Where am I?" I said. My own voice was hoarse and raspy. My throat hurt as if I'd been screaming. I probably had been. "Who are you? Where are my parents? Why are you doing this to me?"

Chunky and Rat Face looked at each other. Chunky shrugged. Rat Face laughed.

"'Where am I?'" he mimicked me. "What do you think, we're idiots? You think we're gonna fall for that?"

"I mean it," I said. "I don't know where I am. I don't know what's happening. Why are you doing this to me? I haven't done anything to you."

I lifted my foot up and down, up and down. *Never give in.*

Chunky stepped up close to the chair and looked down at me. "You're still being smart with us?" he said. "Didn't I show you what happens to smart punks? Didn't you learn anything?"

"Come on, we oughta do this," Rat Face told him nervously.

"I swear," I said desperately. "The last thing I remember, I was at home, I was in bed. I swear."

Anger surged into Chunky's face. He grabbed the front of my shirt. He pulled back his fist.

"Say that again," he said. "I dare you."

I looked up at him. I didn't say it again.

"Come on, come on, come on," said Rat Face. "Prince is waiting. Let's do this, let's go."

Chunky held me another second, his fist raised,

daring me to speak. I didn't. Finally, he smiled his stupid smile. He let go of my shirt front, pushing me back hard. He sneered down at me in triumph. Oh yeah, he was satisfied with himself, all right. He'd ordered me to shut up and frightened me into obeying him. He was a big tough guy, Chunky was. I'll bet he could beat up almost anyone he happened to find strapped to a chair.

I moved my foot up and down. *Never give in.*

Chunky stepped back from me. Rat Face smiled with excitement. Was this it? Were they going to shoot me now?

No. Rat Face turned and moved to the white chest of drawers against the wall.

At that moment, I felt something. A little jolting movement. The strap. The strap on my ankle. I couldn't look at it for fear of drawing their attention to it, but it felt as if it had given way, just a little bit. The metal must've cut into it—just a little bit—but enough so that now I could lift my foot maybe a quarter inch farther, drive it against the metal with just a little bit more force.

Rat Face opened the second drawer in the bureau. My breath caught as he reached in and took out a hypodermic syringe.

He looked over at me. He wanted to see the terror in

my eyes. He did. I was terrified, all right. And he liked that. He liked seeing how scared I was.

"What are you going to do?" I said. The words just came out of me. It wasn't as if I didn't know.

Rat Face took a vial of some clear fluid out of the drawer. He was grinning openly now. Chunky was grinning too.

Rat Face held up the vial so I could see it. "You're gonna like this stuff," he said. "You know what this stuff does? It burns. Yeah. It's, like, some kind of acid or something. I inject this into you and it burns right through you from the inside. Slow, slow, slow. I've seen guys scream for an hour before it killed them. Oh yeah. They scream and scream like you wouldn't believe."

I pretended to go wild with fear. I didn't have to pretend much.

"I don't know anything!" I shouted. "I don't even know where I am!"

I pulled and thrashed against the straps—not really trying to break out, but just because it helped disguise the fact that I was bringing my right foot up harder and harder, and the strap—I could feel it!—the strap was giving way. The metal was cutting into it, deeper and deeper.

Chunky laughed to see my terror. "You should've

talked when you had a chance, you dumb punk," he said. "Look at you now."

Rat Face brought the hypodermic needle to the top of the vial. He pushed it in and began to draw the clear liquid into the barrel of the syringe.

I leaned far forward in my chair, pretending to stomp my foot in rage so I could bring the strap up even harder against the metal.

"Please! Please!" I shouted. "You have to believe me! I don't know you! I don't know how I got here! I don't know where I am!"

And on that last word, I felt the strap around my ankle break. I couldn't be absolutely sure because I couldn't look at it, but I thought I'd managed to cut it clean through. I tested it, moving my foot away from the chair leg just a little.

Yes. Yes. I'd done it. My right leg was free.

CHAPTER SIX

One Shot

The timing was perfect. Rat Face and Chunky didn't notice. Rat Face was too busy drawing the poison into his syringe, his eyes bright with anticipation of my agony and death. And Chunky was watching it, too, savoring the sight of the deadly liquid flowing into the glass barrel.

And now some faint, small, desperate little breath of hope drifted like a tendril of fresh air through the black reaches of my heart. I know: it was only my leg, one leg. The rest of me was still strapped tightly to the chair. But a martial artist has four weapons—two arms, two legs—and now one of my weapons was free. It was something. It was a chance. At least I wouldn't have to die without a fight.

Never give in.

Now there is another saying Sensei Mike taught me. It was something he heard on a television show about the martial arts, an old show called *Kung Fu.* It was, he said, the first rule of a true martial artist, and it went like this: "Avoid rather than check; check rather than block; block rather than strike; strike rather than hurt; hurt rather than maim; maim rather than kill, for all life is precious."

Turn the other cheek—that's the way we say it in my church. If someone offends you, or tries to start a fight with you, turn the other cheek—try to make peace with him—walk away. Do anything you can rather than fight, rather than hurt someone. That's what Sensei Mike taught me, and I believe in it 100 percent. I would never use the martial arts against someone if I didn't have to. I would walk away from any fight I could, even if people called me a coward.

But turn the other cheek doesn't mean let yourself be killed. It doesn't mean let yourself be ruled by bullies, or stand by and do nothing when big guys are picking on little guys or when men are hurting women. I know my mother wouldn't like to hear me say this, and I know some of my teachers wouldn't like it either, but we have another saying in my church: the truth will set you free. And the truth is, there may come a time when even the most peaceful man alive has to fight or else something truly evil will happen.

For me, I knew that time had come.

I took a breath. In through the nose, out through the mouth, relaxing my body. I figured I had one chance, one shot. I had to make it good.

Rat Face was finished. The syringe was full. He laid the vial down on the bureau. He was holding the syringe with the needle in the air. There was a droplet of clear liquid on the tip of the needle. He was watching it closely, warily. He didn't want it to fall on him.

Chunky's eyes were moving back and forth between the needle and me. He had a look of gleeful anticipation on his stupid face.

"Oh, boy," he said. "This is gonna be so good."

Rat Face grinned and came forward, holding the syringe, watching the syringe, walking slowly and carefully as if he were balancing on a rope. "Get ready, punk," he said in his breathy voice. "You're gonna be screaming like an opera singer in a minute."

He came forward another step. I watched him,

waited. I kept my body relaxed, breathing in, breathing out. Believe me, it wasn't easy. I was so scared, I felt as if my throat was closing shut.

Rat Face carried the needle another step toward me and another. He was close enough now so that I could've lifted my free foot and kicked him—but he wasn't where I wanted him to be. It had to be just right. I only had that one chance.

Rat Face came closer, holding the syringe up. He was just off to my right side. He was reaching for my right wrist with his left hand, ready to take hold of me, ready to inject the poison into me.

"All right, my friend," he said, his eyes gleaming. "This'll only hurt for about an hour. Then you'll be dead."

Chunky laughed stupidly at that. He was watching the whole thing like a kid watching fireworks.

Rat Face took another step. Perfect. He was right where I wanted him.

I snapped my leg up fast and hard, a lightning snap kick that flew up smack between Rat Face's legs. I threw that kick with enough force so that it would've hit him in the chin if nothing had stopped it. But his groin stopped it. The kick landed with full force right where it hurts the most.

It happened so fast—it took them so completely by surprise—that Chunky was still smiling as Rat Face's eyes went wide in agony, as his mouth went open to form an enormous O. Then Rat Face dropped the syringe. It shattered on the floor, the clear liquid spilling out of it with a heart-stopping sizzle.

The smile started to fade from Chunky's face. His stupid eyes looked even stupider. He still hadn't processed what had just happened.

Meanwhile, Rat Face grabbed his middle and doubled over. He bent so low, his head moved right past my hand. That's what I was waiting for.

Straining against the strap that held my wrist, I reached out and grabbed Rat Face by the throat. It was a perfect catch. I got him in a pincerlike grip called the dragon's claw. It held the front of his throat tight, right under his chin. His wide eyes went wider still. His tongue appeared in the open O of his mouth. He made a noise. "Ack," it sounded like. A sickly flush began to rise into his brown cheeks.

About one second had passed since I'd thrown my kick. Finally, Chunky was beginning to realize that things were going wrong.

"Hey . . . " he started.

"Shut up," I said. "Shut up and listen. I can kill him now. You hear me? All I have to do is close my hand, and I'll rip his throat out and he's dead."

"Ack! Ack!" said Rat Face, struggling weakly in my grip.

"What are you doing?" Chunky yelled. "Let go of him! What do you think you're doing?"

Scared now, he started backing away from me, toward the door.

"Take another step and I'll do it!" I said.

"Ack!" said Rat Face, reaching a hand out toward Chunky, trying to tell him not to move.

I looked at Rat Face. He was bent over, clutched in my closed fist, turning darker and darker. His hands flailed in the air as he fought for breath.

"I'm going to count to two and kill you," I told him. "Look in my eyes if you think I'm kidding."

He looked in my eyes. I could see the terror flood his features.

"Undo the strap on my wrist," I told him.

Chunky took another half step backward toward the door.

"Don't even think about it!" I said—and he stopped. I turned back to Rat Face. "One . . . " I said.

Rat Face's frantic hands fumbled their way to the strap on my right wrist. It took him a second to steady his fingers enough to do the job. A second later, the strap came loose.

Heaving the right side of my body up off the chair, I hurled Rat Face across the room. He smashed hard into the chest of drawers and collapsed to the floor. He lay there, panting, clutching his throat with one hand and his midsection with the other.

I started to undo the strap on my left wrist.

Chunky saw his moment. He was stupid—but nobody's that stupid. He turned and ran for the door.

There was nothing I could do to stop him. I just kept working as fast as I could. I got the strap off my left wrist.

Chunky threw open the door and ran out of the room.

I got the strap off my left ankle.

I heard Chunky screaming, "Help! West is getting away! Help!"

I leapt out of the chair. A fierce energy punched through the core of me.

I was free.

I ran to the open door. In another second, I was out of the room. There was Chunky, turning this way and that, shouting and shouting, "Help! West is escaping! Help!"

He turned and we were face-to-face. There was one second in which his mean, stupid features went blank with fear.

Then I hit him. I balled my hand into a tight fist and brought it down on him from the side—a hammer-strike, we call it. It thudded against his temple. His eyes flew up, went white. His legs turned to spaghetti. He dropped to the floor like a marionette with cut strings. He lay there still, unconscious.

But it was too late. His call for help was already being answered. I heard what must've been half a dozen people running toward me—thunderous footsteps getting louder and louder.

I looked around. I was in an empty hallway with solid walls of cinder block. But there, at the end of the hall, was a black square—a window with the panes painted over. That's what I thought it was, at least.

The footsteps got louder and louder. I could hear someone shouting, "Stop him! Don't let him get away!"

I started running for the black square.

CHAPTER SEVEN
My Karate Demonstration

Another flash. Another chunk of the past, of that last day, went bolting through my terrified brain.

It was funny. Now, here, with my life in danger, with guards pounding down the hall to catch me, with terror coursing through me like the blood in my veins—now, the last day I could remember seemed to me a day of peace and calm. Everything blessedly ordinary. Everything blessedly serene.

At the time it happened, though, it was different. At the time it happened, I was scared out of my wits.

It was first period at school, the morning assembly. I was standing backstage in the school auditorium. I was waiting for my karate demonstration to begin. Principal Woodman was onstage at the podium, making the day's announcements before introducing me. I had already changed into my gi. It felt kind of strange to be wearing the loose-fitting fighting uniform here in school. It felt as if I'd forgotten to change out of my pajamas. I kept checking and rechecking the knot in my belt to make sure it wouldn't fall off. It was a black belt—the highest rank I was allowed to reach at my age. There was a red stripe in the center of it to show I was still a junior, under eighteen. I found the sight of the belt—the reminder of my high rank—reassuring. I kept telling myself: *I know what I'm doing. There's no reason to be so nervous.*

But I was nervous. I was as nervous as I'd ever been in my life. I was using every breathing and focus technique Sensei Mike had ever taught me, trying to keep myself relaxed and calm and ready—and it still wasn't enough. "It's all right to have butterflies in your stomach," Sensei Mike told me once, "but you've got to make them fly in formation." In other words, marshal your nervous energy to give your techniques extra force. That was easy enough to say, but just then it felt as if my butterflies were crazy out of control, rollicking around in any looney-tune way that happened to strike their butterfly fancy. I wasn't sure I was going to be able to perform my *kata*. To be honest, I wasn't sure I was going to be able to walk out onstage.

The trouble was this: I could see her. Beth Summers, I mean. I could look out through a gap in the curtains and see her sitting there in the front row. The other two class officers were sitting to the left of her: class president Jim Sizemore—hyper-smart but way too full of himself—just beside her, and the ever-nerdy-but-occasionally-hilarious Zach Miliken, the treasurer, in the next seat over.

Beth was turned away from them. She was turned to her right. That's where her friends were sitting. Marissa Meyer and Tracy Wynne. Marissa had long straight dark hair and a perfect oval of a face, like a girl in a portrait. Tracy's hair was also long and straight but golden blonde, and her face was shaped like a valentine. They were both beautiful, two of the prettiest girls in school. Pretty, smart, mega-popular. Heads of about a hundred school organizations and charity projects, not to mention captain of the volleyball team (Marissa) and chief cheerleader (Tracy).

They were nothing compared to Beth, though. Not to

me anyway. There was something special about Beth, about the way she looked, about the way she talked, about the way she just was. Whenever she was around, I couldn't take my eyes off her. I couldn't say why, exactly. She wasn't glamorous or anything, not like her two friends. Her hair was a sort of ordinary honey brown. It was curly and fell to about her shoulders, framing her face in waves and ringlets. Her eyes were blue. Her features were smooth and straight. Her figure, in a knee-length skirt and a pink sweater, was graceful. But there was something else, something more, that made me stand backstage and peer out at her, getting more and more nervous as the moment for me to do my karate in front of her got closer and closer.

It was just how nice she was, I guess. You could see it whenever she smiled, hear it whenever she talked. Marissa and Tracy—they weren't mean or anything. But they weren't like Beth. Beth was always warm and interested in what you were saying. She made you feel like you were the only person in the world she cared about. And I'd never known her to say a cruel thing either—not once, not to anyone, not even to her little brother, Arthur, who was a complete pain and totally deserved it.

Anyway, I'm going on and on about her, I know. But

she really was nice, and it made her beautiful, more beautiful even than the others. So I stood backstage, peeking out through the gap in the curtains and just kind of gazing at her like I was some kind of big stupid dog, or some big stupid something, anyway. And the more I gazed at her, the more nervous I felt. Because I had this sneaking suspicion that I was about to walk out on that stage and make a total idiot of myself right there in front of her. I could just feel it: I hadn't had time to practice, and I was going to make some stupid mistake or split my pants or fall smack on my pratt or something. And I could already picture the way she'd look at me—nicely, you know, but with pity in her eyes. She would pity me while all her friends and all the other kids around her laughed and laughed.

All at once, I came out of my trance and realized that Principal Woodman had begun to introduce me. Of course, that didn't mean I would have to go on right away or anything. Mr. Woodman never said something with a single word if he could say it with ten. Plus he stammered, making every word seem like ten anyway. And he never said anything right the first time and always had to go back over it a second time and correct it. So I figured I still had a few seconds at least—a few seconds left before I went out there and made a fool of myself in front of Beth and everyone else.

"We have a spectral tree for you today," said Principal Woodman. "A special, I mean, a special tree—a treat—a special treat for you. A special treat." He was a tall, thin, pale guy with thin reddish hair and a kind of dopey smile stuck permanently on his face. Whenever he spoke, his body waved back and forth behind the podium like a sapling in a breeze. "Our own Harley—Charlie—what am I talking about?—why did I say Harley?—Charlie— Charlie West is here today—as always—I mean, he's always here, of course, he goes to school here—but today he has a spectral treat in store for us. He's going to—not spectral—special—why do I keep saying spectral?—a special treat—and he's here and he's going to perform some judo." He glanced over his shoulder, through the gap in the curtains, to where I stood backstage. "Or is it karate, Charlie? Karate. Not judo. He's going to perform some karate in a spectral . . ."

Well, I won't tell you the whole thing. It went on like that for another few minutes. And with every word, I felt my butterflies going crazier and crazier and my muscles getting tighter and tighter until I thought I was just going to go out onstage and stand there shivering like a plucked string. I tried to distract myself with getting ready. I pulled my three heavy cinder blocks closer to my feet. I pushed my elbows back, stretching out my shoulders. I forced myself to take deep breaths, in and out, in and out.

Finally, Woodman said, "So here he is—Harley—Charlie West."

There was loud applause, even some cheering. I picked up two of the cinder blocks, one in each hand, and carried them out onstage.

It took me a few seconds to position the blocks on the stage floor. I set them up to the far right, directly in front of where Beth was sitting. The cinder blocks were part of my grand finale, and I wanted her to have a good view of it.

While I was setting the blocks up, the applause died down. Now there was just a nerve-racking silence in the auditorium and the sound of me adjusting the blocks on the floor. When I was done, I had to go backstage again to get the third block. By the time I came out, I could hear the audience fidgeting in their seats and murmuring to one another. They were already bored.

I felt a line of sweat run down my back—and I hadn't even started my kata yet.

Then someone—Josh Lerner, probably—shouted

out, "Go get 'em, Harley-Charlie!" and everyone laughed and I laughed with them, but I felt my cheeks get hot.

I forced myself not to look at Beth to see if she was laughing too. As coolly as I could, I laid the third cinder block across the top of the other two. Then I walked to the podium where Mr. Woodman had been. I had to clear my throat before I spoke, and the sound went into the microphone and came out sounding like a roll of thunder. There was more laughter and more heat in my cheeks and another line of sweat rolling down my back.

When I finally got some words out, I could hear the quaver of nervousness in my voice. I could only hope no one else could hear it.

"I'm gonna do a kata," I said. "It's kind of like a make-believe fight where you imagine different people attacking you and you do defense techniques on them. That way you get to practice your techniques in motion so your muscles will learn how to do them. Then, if you ever have to use the technique in real life, your body will just know how to do it. You won't have to think about it or anything. Anyway, I'm gonna do one now called the Tiger Kata because it uses really powerful striking techniques, which, in my karate school, we call tiger techniques."

Then, for good measure, I cleared my throat into the microphone again, making another thundery noise and getting a few more giggles.

I forced myself to move away from the protection of the podium and walked to the center of the stage. About a thousand cringe-making scenarios were flashing through my mind, a thousand different and excruciating ways in which I might embarrass myself forever. Maybe I would fall off the stage. Maybe I would sprain my ankle and have to hop around like a cartoon rabbit. Maybe my pants would just fall down. Maybe they'd fall down while I was hopping around . . .

I forced the thoughts away. I arranged myself into what's called the front position: feet together, arms lifted in front of me, hands together just in front of my chin. My right hand was in a fist to represent the power of the *yang*, or masculine principle; the left hand was open and covered the fist to represent the restraint of the *yin*, or feminine principle. Power through self-discipline: that's what karate is all about.

I stood like that for a long second. The auditorium had grown really quiet. There was no more shifting around, no more murmuring, no more cracks from Josh Lerner. They were interested, I could tell.

I took one more long breath, and then I went into my salutation.

Right away, a wonderful thing happened, an amazing thing. A salutation begins every kata. It starts with a bow and then a series of motions performed with the muscles very tense and the breath coming through the open mouth with a long, loud hiss. The breath is called Dragon-Breathes-Fire. It's meant to focus your attention and push all your unnecessary thoughts out of you and bring all your energy to bear on the form. And the wonderful, amazing thing that happened is: it did exactly what it was supposed to do. The minute I tensed my abdominal muscles and pushed the dragon breath out of me, all the nervousness flowed out of me too. Suddenly, I had no extra thoughts to spare on anything at all—not even on Beth Summers. Suddenly, there was only the kata—the form—which I knew so well I could do it without thinking—without thinking but not without concentration. And that's the way it was: suddenly, every thought was gone and all my mind was concentrated on performing the kata's movements exactly right.

Which I did. I practically flew across the stage in long animal leaps, ending with mighty strikes in the air where my imaginary opponents were supposed to be.

My fists corkscrewed out and back almost too fast for the eye to follow. My openhanded strikes slashed back and forth in lightning-speed combinations. I kicked and spun and kicked again, then leapt into the air with my body nearly horizontal to drive a devastating flying kick into an imaginary opponent's head. I fell to the earth with a downward finishing strike—a punch spiraling straight to the floor as my body dropped down behind it to give it extra force. I let out a deafening roar— "*keeyai!*"—expelling every ounce of tension in my body, letting the tension explode into the punch as my knuckles scraped the surface of the polished wood.

Then I was upright again, spinning again, lashing out with a hook kick that brought my foot snapping around behind me and the rest of my body snapping around after it. Under the sound of my movements, I could hear the silence of the audience, I could feel their attention on me, feel them caught up in the violent grace of the form. Now I dove forward and went into a rolling somersault. Then I snapped to my feet with a combination of knife-hand strikes and a spinning back kick that brought me around 180 degrees. Someone in the audience—a guy, I'm not sure who—let out a whoop of appreciation, and the rest of the audience applauded. But even then—even as I began to realize that I was doing the best form I'd ever done—even as I began to understand that every eye in the auditorium was locked onto me in fascination—even then, I didn't let it break through my unthinking concentration. I was deep inside myself, deep inside the form. I had no thoughts—just movement, just concentration. Striking, spinning, kicking as fast as I could but keeping every strike forceful, every position absolutely precise.

Now I was ready to perform the final move of the kata—and the most dangerous. I had come to rest on the far left side of the stage, as far from where Beth was sitting as I could get. I was in a crane position, absolutely still with one leg lifted, the knee up to my waist, the foot pointing down, the edge of one open hand hovering above the thigh, the other hand up to block my face. In one more second, I was going to explode out of the crane and drive across the stage behind a flurry of kicks and blows. At the last second, I would leap into the air above the place where the concrete cinder blocks stood, the two standing upright and the third lying across the top. As I came down, I would unleash a driving downward strike—right into the top of that third concrete block. If I did it just right, with all my focus and all my force—if I concentrated my mind on driving not into the concrete but straight through it—I would break the cinder block in two with my bare fist. That was the plan anyway. My fists were well conditioned and I'd broken blocks before—it's not really as hard as it looks.

Still, as I stood there on one leg, poised to begin that final movement, a terrible thought broke through my concentration. I had an image of myself driving downward toward the concrete block—driving downward and then, just at the final second, losing my focus. Too late to pull back, I would continue the driving downward strike into the block—but without the full force of my mind and will behind it, it was not the concrete that would shatter, but every bone in my hand. That was it, I realized suddenly. That was how I was going to make a fool of myself in front of Beth. I was going to drive down into the block and break my hand in a million pieces so that my powerful, roaring *keeyai* would be transformed on the spot into a high-pitched howl of agony. I would go hopping across the stage, gripping my jellylike hand, screaming and screaming while everyone stared in horror and secret amusement. Maybe my pants would even fall off for good measure.

A wavering line of cold nausea went up through the center of me, like a tendril of smoke drifting toward the ceiling. The second the thought of failure occurred to me, I knew I should've changed course and abandoned the grand finale. Without confidence, you can't put your fist through concrete—it just isn't possible. And with a thought like mine in your head, how could you have any confidence at all?

I told myself to force the thought away. I *did* force the thought away, but I knew it was still there, just below the surface. And there was no way I was changing course, no way I was going to quit now. Not with everyone watching. Not with Beth watching.

I hung there poised one more second. I let the breath flood out of my body, hoping it would carry the thought of failure away with it. Then I launched the final sequence.

It all seemed to happen fast and slow at once. I could sense and see that I was moving with unstoppable speed, but my mind was so focused on every moment that it felt like slow motion somehow, like a slow-motion movie unfolding frame by graceful frame. Every kick and blow and step carried me farther and farther across the stage, closer and closer to the cinder blocks. Then I pushed off the floor and was airborne, sailing across the final few yards with my right fist drawing back and back, pressed tight to my side, ready to explode downward as I dropped back to Earth, dropped back to the cinder block.

I was screaming before I thought to scream, the roaring *keeyai* tearing out of the center of me, bursting from me like a tiger bursting out of a cage. I saw the gray of the concrete block rushing up toward me. My mind went down to meet it, went through it. And at the same moment my knee touched the floor, my fist drove out from my side, corkscrewing to where my focus was, on the other side of the cinder block, on the other side of all that concrete.

I don't remember the meeting of flesh and stone. It was as if I had become so much a part of the moment that I could no longer see it. The next thing I knew, shards of concrete were flying up around my face, and the cinder block, smashed into two pieces, was dropping heavily to the floor on either side of my extended arm.

Only slowly did the rest of the world make its way back into my consciousness. By then, I was already drawing myself up, drawing myself out of that last punch and into the movements of my final salutation. I gathered myself again into the front position, my feet together, my arms up in front of me, my right fist covered by my left hand just beneath my chin. Power through self-discipline. I was done.

That was when I heard them, saw them: the students and teachers in the auditorium. They were on their feet, all of them. They were clapping as hard as they could. Some of the guys were hammering the air with their fists. Some of the girls had covered their mouths with their hands. And then all of them were clapping and screaming and cheering as I stood in front of them, bringing my breath under control.

I let my eyes shift to the right, just a little, just enough to get a glimpse of her. Beth had covered her open mouth with both hands. For another second or two, her eyes remained wide with fear and horror, as if she were still waiting to see what would happen when I struck the block. But now she let the hands fall. She took a deep breath of relief. She laughed. The fear and horror went out of her eyes and something else came into them, something I can't describe but could feel flowing through me like a warm river.

Then Beth was applauding too, shaking her head with amazement and laughing and applauding, taking her eyes from me to look at Marissa and Tracy and shaking her head at them in amazement just as they were shaking their heads at her right back.

Slowly, I let my hands drop from front position to

hang at my sides. I nodded my head sheepishly to acknowledge the cheers.

Nice going, Harley-Charlie, I thought to myself.

The audience went on clapping and cheering, and Beth went on clapping and cheering for a good long time, it seemed like.

It was just a day, you know. Just another ordinary September day. But I remembered now—it flashed through my mind: that moment—that moment standing on the stage while Beth and everybody clapped and cheered—which was, I have to admit, one of the coolest moments of my life so far.

CHAPTER EIGHT

The Black Square

Now that moment seemed a lifetime ago—an impossible lifetime that had somehow vanished into nothingness—there in a flash and just as suddenly gone. Beth was gone and my friends and my school and Principal Woodman and my moment of glory—all of it, the whole world I knew, the only world I knew, was gone, and the only cinder blocks around were in the walls of this prison hallway. There was nothing else—nothing I could make sense of—except the pain racking my body and the stampede of footsteps as the guards closed in on me—and that black square, that one black square of hope, coming closer up ahead.

I ran for the black square. I told myself again it was a window that had been painted over. It had to be a window. What else could it be?

It didn't matter. I had to believe there was a way out. I had no other choice. The footsteps behind me were getting louder and louder, closer and closer, and I could hear shouts and curses now and a deep growl of a voice giving the order to "Go, go, go, get him, go, go, go!"

I ran as hard as I could, drove toward the black square, stretching my legs, pumping my arms, putting aside the pain that burned like fire in every part of my body. That black square: It was just like the cinder block at school, I told myself. It was no different from the cinder block. I just had to drive my mind through it, drive my mind straight through to the other side of it. Then my body would follow. At least I hoped it would.

The square kept looming larger as I kept getting closer, but still—still—I couldn't see—couldn't be sure—if it was a window or just some black paint slopped onto the surface of the concrete.

I was almost there, just a few strides away. I glanced back over my shoulder. For another half second the hall was empty—empty except for the big lump of chunky thug still lying unconscious on the floor where I had dropped him.

Then the guards came careering around the corner. I caught a glimpse of the first two—two men—dark, Middle Eastern-looking—both dressed the same, dressed the same as I was in black pants and a white shirt. They were carrying those machine guns, those automatic rifles you see on TV all the time: Kalashnikovs, they're called—AK-47s. They were carrying them in their hands with the straps around their shoulders. As they spotted me, those first two guards dropped to their knees. They brought the rifles to bear. Two more men had already come around the corner behind them. They leveled their rifles also, pointing them at me above the heads of the first two. Four guns were trained on my back.

There was no more time to watch. I faced forward. The black square was now only a half step away. I threw myself at it headlong, full force.

The guards opened fire. Terror flashed through me. The stuttering coughs of the AKs seemed to drown out everything, every hope of survival, every thought of anything but death. Chips of concrete flew everywhere. My heart seized up at the stinging whine of ricochets. And then part of the black square shattered—a glass pane: it was a window after all!

The very next instant my body hit it. My arms were crossed over my face, my head was turned away. I hit the black square with my shoulder, struck the window's sash with jarring violence. The sash snapped and gave way.

There was a long, tumbling moment of fear and singing bullets and the coughing Kalashnikovs and the breaking wood and glass.

Then I hit the ground—hard. The impact made my bones ache. Glass and wood rained down on top of me. Bullets whispered by overhead.

After the dark hall, the sunlight was blinding. The air was cool and fresh and filled my gasping lungs. I felt an unreasoning surge of hope and crazy joy. I was out—out of the prison—out in the open air!

But there was no time to think about that. Already I was rolling away from the window, fighting to lift myself to one knee. Already I heard more of those thunderous footsteps inside the building behind me, the prison I'd just broken out of. I heard more shouts: "Don't let him get away! Let's go—go!"

Dazed and stupid with panic, I knelt on the hard earth and looked around. I was in a broad compound of some sort. I saw gray barrack-style buildings. A fence with barbed wire on top. Guard towers rising against the forest behind them. Inside the towers: men with guns.

Somewhere, an alarm bell started ringing. Out of the corner of my eye, I saw red lights begin to whirl and flash. I heard those guards shouting: "Get him!" Those thundering footsteps. The roar of an engine . . .

An engine. Where? My eyes wide with fear, I turned toward that roar. I saw a big old pickup truck bouncing over the rough ground near me. I caught a glimpse of the man behind the wheel. He seemed oblivious to the emergency unfolding around him. The alarm and shouts and whirling lights hadn't reached him yet, hadn't registered on his brain. He was still relaxed, steering the truck with one hand, leaning the other arm on the frame of the open window. The truck was heading toward a gate in the fence, the exit of the compound. The guards there were swinging the gate open to let him out. They were just now pausing, just now trying to figure out what all the noise and fuss were about.

All this I took in in a single second. In the next second, I had to act—had to act without even thinking.

I ran at the truck. Just as it passed me, I leapt at the window.

I caught hold of the window frame. The driver—a square-jawed white guy in his forties, maybe—turned to me in stunned surprise, his jaw dropping, his mouth a wide O.

There was no running board, nothing to rest my feet on. There was nothing I could do now but grip the frame of the open window and try to pull myself inside. With all the wild force of my terror, I yanked myself halfway through the window. I heard the driver curse. He swung the wheel. I felt the truck swerve hard, lifting up on one side. I clawed my way over him, into the cab.

The truck swerved again. The driver cursed again as I tumbled in on him. He tried to punch at me, but I was right on top of him. We were too bunched up together for him to get any force into the blow. His fist beat weakly at my shoulder. I wouldn't have felt it at all except for the fact that I was already bruised and burned and beaten, already in so much pain.

But that didn't stop me. I was in the truck now, sliding over the driver, falling into the passenger seat.

I caught a quick glimpse of the scene racing by outside the window. I saw the guards with their Kalashnikovs come storming out of the prison barracks in which I'd been held. They were all shouting at one another. One of them was pointing here and there, giving orders to take up positions. Another one was lifting his rifle, training it on the truck. But he couldn't get a shot at me, not without killing the driver.

But the driver . . . he had a gun of his own. It was a sidearm, a pistol, in a holster on his belt. He was driving with his left hand now, reaching for the gun with his right, unsnapping the flap of the holster to get at it.

He hadn't taken his foot off the gas. He kept the truck going full speed. He wrenched the wheel, trying to keep me off balance while he drew the gun.

It worked. Balled up on the seat next to him, I was thrown hard against the dashboard, then thrown back against the seat. I reached out my hand to brace myself against the dash, to steady myself. The driver had his holster open now. His hand closed around the handle of his gun. He started to draw it out.

I pulled my knees tight into my chest, then shot both legs out in front of me. I landed a powerful double kick to the side of the driver's head.

I heard him grunt above the engine's roar as the double blow struck him. The truck swerved again, lifting up so high on one side this time that I thought for sure it would turn over. The driver's gun hand flew up in the air.

The pistol flew out of his grip, bouncing off the back of the cab, sailing back past me to drop onto the cab floor.

Quickly, I squirmed my body around, going after the gun. I reached down. I felt it. I grabbed it.

I was thrown against the dashboard again as the truck lurched suddenly to a stop. I struggled to sit up while the driver sat still behind the wheel, shaking his head, dazed.

I grabbed his shirt collar. I put the gun against his temple.

"Get out!" I shouted.

The truck had now pulled up next to one of the barracks at the far edge of the compound—far, I mean, from the prison barracks where I'd started out. Out the window, I could see the armed guards rushing across the compound toward us. The driver looked at me sideways, angry, confused.

"Get out now!" I shouted, pushing the gun up hard against his head.

That reached him. Frightened, he fumbled for the handle of the door. The guards outside saw the door opening and pulled up short. They lifted their AKs.

As soon as the door cracked open, I gave the driver a hard shove. He was big, but he was still dazed from the kick to the head. He went tumbling out the door like a side of beef and dropped hard onto the ground. Even as he was falling, I was sliding into his place behind the wheel.

With the driver out of the way, the guards outside had a clear shot at me. I saw them lifting their rifles again, pointing them at the open door of the truck.

But now I had the steering wheel in my hands. I had the gas pedal under my foot. There was no time to close the door. I just hit the gas.

The truck jolted forward. The door swung wide, hit its limit, and bounced back, slamming shut. At the same moment, the guards outside opened fire. I heard the deadly sputter of their guns above the engine's roar. I heard the bullets ripping into the steel of the truck. I couldn't see where they hit. I didn't plan to wait around and find out.

I floored the pedal. I wrenched the wheel. The scenery outside—the fence, the towers, the barracks, the guards—it all went into a swirling blur as the truck turned and turned. I caught sight of the compound gates, the guards standing beside them. I pulled the wheel back over. Dust flew up on every side of me as the truck righted itself and shot forward.

A cloud of dust rolled up over the windshield. I peered through it desperately, trying to see the way. Dimly, the world outside took shape again. There were the gates, there were the gate guards. Only seconds had passed since I'd broken out of the barracks. The two guards had been swinging the gates open to let the truck out. The gates were still open—or half-open, anyway. As I drove the truck toward them, I saw the two guards frantically trying to push them shut again.

The engine roared and I roared, my eyes peering through the dust, pinned to the closing gates. As the truck sped toward him, one of the guards let his gate go. He left it half-open and turned to level his machine gun at me.

The next moment, a jagged bullet hole appeared in the windshield, a spiderweb network of cracks instantly stretching out on every side of it. I heard the bullet sing past my ear. I heard it rip into the back of the cab just behind my head.

Panicked, I wrenched the wheel again, but before the truck could get out of the line of fire, I guess another bullet must've struck because now the windshield shattered completely.

The truck was turning as it hit the gates. It hit off

center, but that seemed to help somehow: the hood shoved the half-open gate open wide. I stomped on the gas again. The truck let out another throaty roar and fired forward through the gates and out of the compound.

This is what I saw in that next insane, panicked, terrified second. I saw a dirt road leading through a small field of grass and wildflowers. I saw the field end in forest—what looked like deep forest that went on a long, long way. I saw the dirt road become a dirt trail that vanished among the trees. I saw the blue sky and big, lofty clouds blowing by over the treetops.

I wrenched the wheel one more time, straightening the truck on the dirt road. I sped toward the trailhead, toward the protection of the forest.

I never made it.

The road was rough. There were deep holes in the dirt. Big rocks strewn about everywhere. It wasn't a road made for fast travel. And I was traveling fast—very fast—as fast as that truck could go. The pedal was hard against the floor. My speed was increasing with every second. The cool air was streaming in on me through the broken windshield, and so was the blinding dust. Grass and white wildflowers, meadow and woods and sky were rushing by the windows on either side. The truck was bouncing crazily, lifting up high on every rock, dropping down hard, diving and jolting with a sickening crunch into each new hole.

I didn't care. I paid no attention. I never touched the brakes. I never let up on the gas. I could still hear the rattling coughs of those machine guns behind me—at least I thought I could—that sound was stuck in my imagination now. I could hear it in my mind, anyway, and I could practically feel the bullets flying after me, searching out my flesh, trying to tear into me, to tear me apart. All I wanted was to get to those trees. That's all I cared about. To get into the darkness of the woods before the guards and their guns caught up with me.

But it was no good. It was too fast—too fast for that road, those rocks, those holes. I was too wild with panic, too desperate and afraid to keep control of that speeding truck for long.

It was a rock that did it in the end. A great, flat gray rock hidden in the rough dirt road until the last minute. I saw it only a split second before my left front tire hit it with full force. At that speed, that was all it took. The pickup lifted into the air. The steering wheel became useless in my hands. I wrenched it to the side, tried to land the truck again, but it made no difference. I had no control. The truck went over. It hit the ground with a force that made my eyes rattle. The next thing I knew, it was turning over and over, hurling me this way and that inside the cab.

Instinctively, I let go of the wheel. I threw my arms up to protect my head. There was nothing now but nauseating chaos. I caught glimpses of the trees turning sideways through the jagged frame of the broken windshield. I saw the sky turning and the clouds turning and everything rolling over and over. My body was smashed against the ceiling, then against the door, and then thrown sideways across the passenger seat.

Then it was finished. The truck lay still. There was silence—only it wasn't really silence—it was just my own muddied consciousness, too shocked and battered to take in anything going on outside. I don't know how long I was like that. Not long, I guess. It was probably just a few seconds before my mind began to clear, before the sounds of the world started to come back to me. They were the same sounds as before, the same sounds that seemed to have been surrounding me for hours now, maybe forever. The sound of the chattering rifles, the sound of shouting—"Get him! Go!"—the sound of running footsteps, muffled now as my pursuers left the compound and came toward me across the meadow.

I lay in the cab of the truck, dazed. I lay there and listened to the sounds. The sounds made me feel—I don't know—very sad and very tired somehow. I felt much too tired to do anything, to try to run anymore or fight or escape. I just wanted all these evil people to go away. I just wanted them to leave me alone. I wanted to be home again, back in my own house, in my own bed, waiting half-awake for my mom to call upstairs and tell me it was time to get ready for school. Why were these people hurting me? Why were they after me? How could I stop them? I was just a kid. I lay there in the cab of the over-turned truck and I just wanted to break down and cry with weariness and frustration.

Lazily, my head rolled to one side. My vision seemed dull. The world seemed covered with shadows. Through those shadows, I could make out the light of day. I could make out the scene through the truck window. The world out there seemed to be very far off. It seemed as if it had nothing to do with me.

There they were. Same as before. Those men. Those men running after me. Those men with rifles coming to get me, coming to drag me back to the compound and strap me back in that chair and shoot that poison into me and watch me scream and scream until I was dead.

There they were. Coming closer every second.

And I was just too tired, too sick, too beaten to go on running anymore.

CHAPTER NINE

Lunch

Lying there, my spirit broken, my mind flashed back in time again, my heart went home. A series of images swam swiftly through my dazed brain. That last morning . . . my karate demonstration . . . Beth . . . Alex . . .

It seemed now like a sweet, simple time: the last good day. It seemed now that my life had been perfect then. I had food to eat, and a house to live in, parents to take care of me. I lived in a wonderful, free country where I could say what I wanted and do what I wanted and be anything I had the talent to be. No one was shooting at me or beating me up or strapping me to chairs and trying to inject acid into me. I should have woken up every morning and thanked God for his blessings. I should have headed off to school each day whistling a happy tune.

But at the time, it didn't seem like that at all. At the time, I thought I had plenty to worry about—plenty. I mean, I was in high school, for one thing. What could be more worrisome than that? For another thing, this was the year I had to take calculus. It was insanely hard, and I worried it would wreck my grade point average. And if it didn't, there was Mr. Sherman, my history teacher, to worry about. I thought he was out to get me because I argued with him all the time, and a lot of the time I won. For instance, he stood up in class once and said all these nasty things about America. He said America was racist and violent and greedy. So I just got up and told him that he was wrong and that the facts proved him wrong. I told him, sure, people in America make mistakes because people everywhere make mistakes. But when you came right down to it, there was not one place on Earth where people had any freedom or dignity or human rights and

America hadn't helped it happen or helped it stay that way. I challenged him to name one place—one single place on Earth—and he couldn't, because there isn't one. Ever since then, I'd been getting lower grades on my papers for his class.

So that made me worry I wouldn't get into a decent college. And that made me worry I couldn't fulfill my secret ambition in life, which I hadn't told anyone because I worried it would make my mother's head explode in terror and because I wasn't even sure it was realistic any-way—and I worried about that too.

And maybe more than anything, I worried about Beth Summers. Whom I couldn't stop thinking about and who seemed kind of impossibly out of my league. Every time she even got close to me, I started to sound as if my IQ had dropped forty points and someone had superglued my tongue to the top of my mouth. "Heddo, Bet, it gud to tee you." Plus there was a rumor that she had kind of a thing for someone else and that he had kind of a thing for her—and that this someone else was Alex Hauser, who happened to technically still be my best friend.

Josh Lerner had passed this story on to me in his IM guise as the supremely irritating GalaxyMaster. He said that this past summer, when both Alex and Beth had been working part-time at the Main Street Blender-Benders, they had become good friends. They'd started walking home after work every day, and Alex had talked to her about his folks splitting up and all the trouble in his life. Of course, Beth had listened to him in that way she had that made you feel like you were the only person on Earth. So Alex had fallen for her because . . . well, who wouldn't?

The way GalaxyMaster told it, Beth had sort of fallen for Alex, too, really developed a crush on him. But that was about the time when Alex started hanging out with the jerks he was hanging out with, and doing the stuff he was doing and talking the way he was. Egged on by his new buds, he'd started getting rude and creepy with Beth, pushing himself on her and bothering her to do a lot of stuff she didn't want to do. Well, you can figure it out for yourself.

Anyway, the upshot was—so the story went—that Beth told Alex she didn't like the way he was acting and Alex said fine, what did he care, there were plenty of other girls around, and so have a nice life and good riddance. And he stormed off. And Beth realized that was for the best, but she was still really sad about it because she really did have a thing for Alex, and she felt as if her heart was broken.

That was the story, anyway, according to Galaxy-Master. And I have to admit it made things with Beth a bit more complicated. See, Alex and I had known each other since we were in kindergarten, and we'd been best friends for a long time. For years, he spent practically every Saturday at my house, and when he wasn't there, I was at his. We rode bikes together. Played ball together. For a while, Alex had even taken karate lessons with me. Then he'd gotten more into baseball and joined the Legion League and didn't have time for karate. But that was okay. We were still friends, we'd still hang out together and go for hikes or to the movies or whatever.

Then, about a year ago, after a lot of arguments and yelling and crying all around, Alex's dad moved out. Not just out of the house either. He moved to a whole different city. His mom didn't have as much money as before, and she and Alex and his brother had to move to another part of town. That meant Alex had to change schools, too, so we hardly saw each other at all. After a while, Alex even stopped coming by my house on the weekends. In fact, he pretty much stopped talking to me altogether. I mean, I'd try to make contact. I'd call him. I'd e-mail. I'd even drop by his new place, even though it was almost forty minutes by bike. But Alex didn't seem interested in talking to me anymore. He didn't just ignore me. He kind of snorted and rolled his eyes when he saw me coming. He practically told me to go away and leave him alone. So I did leave him alone. But I sent him one last e-mail. It said, basically: *Look, I know you're going through a hard time, but just so you know, I'm still your friend and if you want to talk about it or just hang or whatever, you know where I am.* I still hoped he'd take me up on the offer because he was always a good guy and I missed seeing him.

Now, look, I wasn't going to *not* ask Beth out because it might annoy Alex. She could make her own decisions and he could fend for himself. But it was just one more thing to worry about, if you see what I mean. Not to mention the little matter of working up my courage to talk to Beth in the first place.

But that problem, strange to say, suddenly solved itself.

It happened right after my karate demonstration. I was feeling good. In fact, after the way everyone clapped and cheered for me, I was feeling really good. *Really.* Everyone was coming up to congratulate me. People would start clapping again when they saw me walking past in the halls. Guys were giving me approving punches in the shoulder as I walked past, and girls . . . well, maybe it was my imagination, but they just seemed to be looking at me a little differently, smiling at me a little more and so on. Breaking a cinder block with your fist may not be the most useful skill you can develop, but it sure seems to impress people. Even Mr. Sherman made a joke about it in history class: "Charlie may be a small-minded tool of America's fascist overlords," he said, "but given his self-defense skills, I'm not sure I'd want to say that to his face." Well, whatever.

After Sherman's class, it was time for lunch. I sat at my usual table. Josh Lerner and Rick Donnelly were already there with their brown bags when I approached with my lunch tray. Wednesday was mac 'n' cheese day, the one day I shelled out the extra cash for a hot lunch at school. Rick and Josh looked up from opening their bags long enough to jut out their chins in welcome. At the same time, Kevin Miles—Miler Miles, we call him, because he runs long-distance—joined us with his mac 'n' cheese. We all sat down together, same as always.

"So, dude," Josh said to me. "You are the man of the hour." Josh was a geek and looked pretty much like he'd been made at the Geek Factory: short, hunch-shouldered; big, thick glasses over a constant, nervous smile; a tight head of black curly hair.

"Only next time, you oughta break the cinder block with your forehead," said Rick. Rick had a big cheerful face, dark brown, the color of chocolate. He was one of the tallest guys at school. Tall and so thin, he looked like a big wind would bend him double. But he was actually strong and quick and was one of the best players on the school's basketball team, the Dragons.

"Oh, that would be so cool," said Miler. He drove his head down toward his macaroni tray and made a crashing noise. Miler was a small guy, lean and compact, with short blond hair and a kind of long face with sharp green eyes. I always thought Miler ought to have a little sign on his forehead that said, "I am going to be a corporate lawyer one day and make a gazillion dollars." It was one of those things you could tell just by looking at him.

"Or wouldn't it be cool if, like, you drove your head into a cinder block and it didn't work?" said Josh.

"Hey, thanks a lot," I said.

But Rick laughed. "Yeah. What if you just, like, drove your head into the block and it went, like, splosh, you know, and there'd be, like, brains and blood everywhere."

"Yeah!" said Miler, laughing. "And Mr. Woodman would say, 'Hmm, well, Harley-Charlie, I guess you'll have to practice that move a little more.'"

"Harley-Charlie," said Josh with his trademark snicker. "I loved that. That killed me. What do you say from now on we just call you Harley-Charlie all the time?"

"Hey, Josh," I said. "You remember what happened to that cinder block when I punched it?"

"Yeah."

"Well, what do you say, from now on, you don't call me Harley-Charlie at all?"

"Whoa!" said Rick, and he gave me a high five.

Josh snickered into his ham-and-cheese sandwich.

"You know what else would be cool?" said Miler Miles. We all turned to him to find out. But we never did. Because he didn't say anything else. He just sat there, kind of staring into space.

"Well?" said Josh. He snickered some more. "He's, like, *you know what would be cool*, and we're, like, *what*, and he's, like, just sitting there . . ."

Somewhere during Josh's vivid recap of events, it occurred to me that Miler wasn't just staring into space. He was actually staring *at* something. Or someone. So I turned around to see what it was.

What it was was Beth Summers.

She had come up right behind me. She was just standing there—I guess she was waiting for a chance to get my attention. She had her purse over one shoulder and her books in her other hand as if she was on her way somewhere else. Which made sense, because she didn't usually have lunch the same period as me.

"Beth!" I blurted out, surprised. I stood up. I'm not sure why I stood up—I just did. I stood up and twisted around out of my chair and faced her.

The guys—Josh and Rick and Miler—all sort of sat there staring up at the two of us, Josh with the words dying on his lips, Rick and Miler with their lips sort of parted. They looked about as stunned as the people in New York City when they looked up and saw King Kong for the first time. It wasn't that Beth was too good or too stuck-up to talk to me or anything. She wasn't like that, not at all. And it wasn't that I was the least popular guy in school either. That would officially be Al Dokler. It was just that she was Beth and I was me, and if I'd told one of these guys she was going to come over to my lunch table to talk to me, he would've said, "Yeah, only in your dreams," and I would've thought, *Yeah—he's right. Only in my dreams.*

But here she was. And there was no point just standing there, staring at her like an idiot. So instead I stood there and stared at her like an idiot and said, "Hi, Beth. What's going on?"

"I just wanted to tell you how cool your thing in assembly was today," she said. And there was that whole nice, warm business I was talking about. The way she said it, as if no one's thing in assembly had ever been cool before.

"Thanks," I said.

"When you came down on that block? When I saw what you were going to do, I was, like, *oh my goodness, he's gonna kill himself,* like, *break his hand into a hundred pieces.* Then, when you actually broke through the block like that, I was, like, so, so relieved." She really sounded like she was so, so relieved too. So, so worried about me, and so, so relieved. It was nice.

"Thanks," I said again. I was really pushing the conversational envelope here.

"Anyway, it was cool. It was really cool," she said.

And guess what I said? "Thanks."

Then she stood there for another second, as if there was something else I was supposed to say. I felt like there *was* something else I was supposed to say, but for the life of me, I couldn't think of what it might be. I didn't want to say thanks again, and I couldn't figure out anything else, so I just did the whole stand-and-stare-like-an-idiot routine again.

Finally Beth raised her free hand and gave that little metronome wave girls give—ticktock, ticktock—and said, "Well . . . I just wanted to tell you that. I'll see you around, okay?"

"Okay," I said. At least it wasn't "Thanks." Then I did some more idiotic standing and staring.

With a smile that registered approximately a 9.5 on the Sweetness Scale, Beth turned and started walking away from me, walking toward the cafeteria door.

"Hey, Beth?" I said. I didn't mean to say it. I didn't even know I was going to say it until I heard the words coming out of my mouth. But somehow I couldn't just let her walk away like that.

Beth stopped at the door. She turned back to me, waiting expectantly. She'd moved far enough away so that I had to take a few steps after her to catch up. That was good with me. It got me away from my table, from the staring eyes and flummoxed expressions of Josh and Miler and Rick.

I came up to stand in front of Beth again. I had that feeling again that there was something I was supposed to say, something she was waiting for. I opened my mouth, but nothing came out. I just stood there with my mouth open for what seemed like about half an hour.

Finally, Beth laughed—not in a mean way, just in a kind of what's-going-on way. "You forget what you wanted to say?" she asked me.

"No. No, I didn't forget," I said. "I just . . . I wanted to say . . . It's just . . . it's just I really like you, Beth."

I couldn't believe I said that. I just blurted it right out. I felt like such an incredible idiot.

But Beth didn't laugh at me or anything. She just kind of opened her eyes wider and looked really surprised. "Oh," she said. "Well, thank you . . ."

I stumbled on quickly, without thinking, because I didn't want there to be any more stupid silences. "The thing is: it makes me really nervous when I talk to you."

She looked even more surprised. "It does?"

"Yeah!" I said. I laughed. It was actually kind of a relief to just say it out loud like that. It was a relief not to try to hide it or to pretend to be cool with her. "I get, like, *really* nervous. I feel like my tongue is superglued to the top of my mouth."

"Agh, I hate when that happens."

"No kidding. I really gotta stop messing with that stuff."

She laughed. She had a nice laugh. "Well, I'm glad you

like me anyway," she said. "I like you too." She actually said that. I swear I'm not making this up.

"Really?" I said. "Cool. So you want to, like, go see a movie together or something?"

It was that easy in the end. Suddenly I'd just said it. Suddenly it was just out there.

And just as suddenly, Beth said, "Sure, that'd be fun. Only nothing scary. I hate scary movies."

"Me too," I said. I don't know why I said that. I love scary movies. It just came out because I guess I wanted to make sure she went on liking me.

"My mom doesn't let me go to them anyway," said Beth. "She says they're disgusting."

"Right, no scary movies. We don't even have to go to a movie at all. We could just get a pizza or something."

"Oh, I love pizza."

"But no scary pizza."

She laughed. "Right. Or we could go see the Dragons play. Anyway, why don't you just call me and we'll figure something out? Here."

She handed her books to me and I held them while she fished a marker out of her purse. Then she took my free hand in one of hers. She wrote her phone number on the back of my hand with her marker.

"That tickles," I said.

"It's a very funny number," she said.

I laughed. While she finished writing, I took the opportunity to study the way her hair fell forward across her face. It was a nice way. Definitely nice.

"There," she said. She gave me my hand back. I gave her back her books. "Your tongue still superglued?" she asked me.

I moved my tongue around in my mouth to check. "What do you know?" I said. "Stuff's not as strong as they say."

"There's no truth in advertising." She shifted her books back under her arm. "Well, I'm really glad I stopped by."

"Me too."

"So I'll see you, right?"

"Right. Definitely. You'll definitely see me."

That's what I thought as I stood there watching her walk away. That I'd see her—definitely. I glanced down at the number written in marker on the back of my hand and I thought: *I'll call her and I'll see her.* Just like that. The way it felt . . . it almost didn't seem real to me. It seemed like something I would daydream. It *was* something I would daydream—that I *had* daydreamed—only I wasn't daydreaming now. It was all real.

Then she went out the door, out of the cafeteria, and she was gone and I never saw her again—never again that I remember, anyway.

Because when I woke up the next day, the daydream was over and I was right in the middle of my worst nightmare.

CHAPTER TEN

Leave Me Alone, Winston Churchill

I lay dazed in the cab of the upside-down pickup truck. I was in the middle of the field, about two-thirds of the distance from the compound to the forest trailhead. The guards with their Kalashnikovs were running across the field toward me.

But I wasn't thinking about them. I was thinking about Beth. Her smile flashed through my mind again, that 9.5-on-the-Sweetness-Scale smile. I saw her as clearly as if she were right there in front of me. I saw her turn her eyes to me. And she spoke! Only it was the weirdest thing. I could see her face, I could see her lips moving. But the voice that came out was not her voice. It was a deep voice—a man's voice—and it had a British accent.

It said: *Never give in.*

I groaned. I shook my head slowly back and forth: no, no, no. I thought: *Leave me alone, Winston Churchill. I'm tired now. I can't do anything more. Leave me alone. Let me talk to Beth.*

I tried to make him go away. I tried just to concentrate on Beth, just to see her there and hear her voice instead of his. But the harder I squinted, trying to hold on to the sight of her face, the more she seemed to fizzle and fade like the TV picture at my house when a strong wind blows tree branches in front of the satellite dish. The image of her became choppy and transparent, and I could look right through her and dimly make out the window of the overturned truck and the upside-down world beyond it and the upside-down meadow out there with its green grass and its white wildflowers—and the upside-down guards with their upside-down guns, running as fast as they could right toward me.

Coming to get me. To drag me back to the compound. To kill me.

Never give in.

There he was again. Whispering insistently in my ear. Bugging me.

Leave me alone, I told him again. *I'm tired. The battle is over. I lost.*

Never, never, never, he answered.

Was this guy the biggest pain in the neck ever or what? Always saying the same thing over and over and over like a broken record. I couldn't imagine how he ever got elected prime minister of Great Britain. He didn't understand. He didn't grasp the complexities of the situation. He didn't know—he couldn't know—how much every bone in my body ached, how every muscle screamed with pain. He couldn't know how tired I was— more tired than I'd ever been in my life—and how dazed and frightened I was after being tortured and shot at and banged around inside this stupid truck. All I wanted was to slip away inside myself and be with Beth again and see her smile and hear her voice.

I tried to explain it to him. *There's nothing else I can do, Winston Churchill*, I said. *This is just the way it is now, okay? Sure, it's kind of sad, them coming to kill me and me being only seventeen and everything. And I wish it weren't happening. I really do. But I mean, it's not my fault! I don't even know how I got here. I don't even know what's going on. I tried my best to get away just like you told me, and I failed. That's all. It didn't work, okay?*

Never give in, said Winston Churchill in my ear. *Never, never, never, never.*

I sighed wearily. *All right*, I thought. *I'll try. It's not going to help, but I'll try.*

Using all my strength, I forced my eyes open wide.

Everything came clear in front of me. I could see that only a second had passed since the truck had rolled over. My memory of Beth—my conversation with Winston Churchill—all this had flashed by in only a moment. The guards were still just coming through the gate of the compound, just beginning to cross the meadow toward me. If I could get myself moving—if I could get myself out of this truck—there might be time—there might just be time for me to make a run for it into the forest and find a hiding place among the trees.

That thought—that hope—sent new strength and energy coursing through me. It gave me strength. I started moving.

The first thing I had to do was twist my body around so I could get out through the window. It wasn't easy. As soon as I started to move, a shock wave of pain radiated

94

through me. Every sinew in my body seemed to have been scorched raw. There seemed no place left inside that wasn't in agony.

Never . . . Winston Churchill started to say.

Yeah, yeah, yeah! I said back to him. *I'm moving, I'm moving.*

And I did move, a ragged cry squeezing out between my gritted teeth as the pain surged through me again.

I twisted around in the upside-down cab and started squirming my way out the open window. I felt as if my muscles were on fire, but even though it made me cry out again, I kept going. I got my hand through the window—got it out onto the earth outside. I dug my fingers into the dirt and pulled myself farther.

Grunting and coughing, I crawled halfway out of the truck. I turned onto my back. Drew up my legs. The rest of me came clear and I rolled over, tumbling away onto my face. As I did that, something fell off me. I heard it land with a soft thud on the grass and looked for it. It was the gun—the pistol the driver had tried to pull on me. I grabbed it. Quickly shoved it into my waistband. Then I was working my way off the ground, up onto my knees.

I looked over the meadow toward the onrushing guards. They were still far away, still too far to get a good shot at me. All I had to do was stand. All I had to do was run. With a little luck, I might just make it into the darkness and protection of the forest.

I was about to give it a try when an idea came to me. I paused, reached back into the truck. I grabbed the keys dangling from the ignition. This was the only vehicle I'd seen in the compound. If they couldn't drive it, they would have to chase me on foot. I'd have a better chance.

I pulled the keys out. I noticed the keychain was one of those black plastic things with the push-button flashlight in it. That might come in handy too. I shoved it into my pocket.

Now it was time. I gritted my teeth again. I had grabbed hold of the side of the truck. I used it to pull myself to my feet, almost sobbing now from the pain. I glanced back at the guards. They had slowed down for a second. I think they were startled to see me moving. They actually stared at me and pointed.

But not for long. Soon they were running toward me again. Now I could hear them shouting to one another, shouting at me: "Stop! Hold it right there!" They were getting close fast. They were leveling their weapons at me.

There was no more time. I had to go. I had to run. No matter how much it hurt, I had to run as fast as I could for that tree line.

Never give in.

I let go of the truck and took off.

It was a strange thing. I knew I'd been tortured, beaten, maybe burned. I knew I'd been roughed up fighting with the driver and knocked around inside the truck as it rolled. The pain all through my body was terrible, and I knew it should've been crippling. I shouldn't have been able to do more than limp a few steps and then fall exhausted to the ground. And at first, it was bad. Worse than bad. It was awful. At first, it felt as if my limbs and my torso were encased in some kind of spiked suit, some kind of torture suit that held me back and stabbed into me every time I tried to move.

Then, though—then—with every new step—the suit somehow seemed to get lighter. Somehow, the faster I went, the lighter it got, until bit by bit, step by step, I was flying over the grass, racing as fast as I could for the trees, and the pain was leaving me as if the torture suit were breaking up and falling off, the pieces of it flying away behind me.

Never, never . . .

All right, Winston Churchill, all right already, do I look like I'm giving in?

I ran. I stuck to the dirt road and ran as hard as I could, racing toward the trailhead and the woods. The wall of trees rose up over me as I got closer. Huge maples and oaks and towering evergreens: the closer I got, the higher they seemed to rise, the more they seemed to block out the sky and the sun that was sinking behind them. Another step and the warm sun was gone, blocked out by the trees completely so that I was running in cool shadow.

I glanced back over my shoulder. The guards were almost at the truck now. One of them had dropped to his knees. He steadied his AK and started shooting at me. The deadly sputter of the gun—that heart-stopping sound—reached me across the meadow and made my stomach turn over with fear. The guard was still too far away to get a clean shot, but that didn't make me feel any better. He didn't need a clean shot. He only needed a lucky one. Every moment, I kept waiting for the bullets to hit me and bring me down.

The fear gave me another burst of energy. I stopped looking back and ran even faster. Now there was nothing in front of me but the trunks of the trees and the deep depth of tangled green darkness that was the forest interior.

Then I felt an earthy cool, and the trees closed over me. The trail turned sharply and I tore along it. I looked back. The guards were lost to view—that meant they couldn't see me either anymore, couldn't get a shot at me at all.

But I didn't slow down for a second. I just kept running. Running on the trail fast as I could. Leaping over holes and roots and rocks. Running deeper and deeper into the welcoming shadows of the forest. Running through the pain. Running for my life.

Never give in.

CHAPTER ELEVEN
The Woods

I don't know how long I ran like that. A long, long time, it seemed like. The woods got thicker and thicker around me, darker and darker as they shut out the sun. I strained my eyes, looking for a sign of civilization. A house, a cabin, a ranger station, anything. But as far as I could see, the woods went on forever, an endless, mysterious pattern of vines and branches, massive tree trunks and low shrub.

For a while, I stuck to the trail. It was broad and flat—more like a fire road than a hiking trail—so I could move along it quickly. I figured that was the best way to put some distance between me and the guards. In here, see, in the forest, their weapons were useless at long range. There was no way they could even see me for any distance, let alone get a shot at me through the trees. So they'd have to catch up to me first. They might be able to do that if they could push a vehicle through here. But if I was right about that truck—if it was the only vehicle in the compound—or even if they had to go back to the compound to get another truck—then I had time to cover some territory before they could begin to close the gap.

So I ran along the trail as fast as I could go, deeper and deeper into the woods. But it was tough going. I was already unsteady, battered, hurt. Soon enough, I began to feel my legs start to weaken and my lungs start to give out. Not to mention, I needed a drink of water—a lot. I didn't know how long it'd been since I'd had a drink, but I was starting to feel the need in a big way—not just in my dusty mouth and my parched throat, but in the wooziness that was seeping into my brain like fog and the weakness that was spreading from the core of me out to my limbs.

Finally, I was staggering. The trail was no good to me now. I couldn't travel quickly anymore anyway. So I left it and plunged into the depths of the brush and trees.

There was no running here, not for long. After just a few steps, the undergrowth got so thick that I had to tear it away with my hands to make any progress at all. On the plus side, the trail was soon invisible behind me, which made me suspect I was probably more or less invisible from the trail as well. Even if the guards caught up to me, they wouldn't be able to see me. They might well miss me and run right past.

But if the way had been hard before, it was even harder now. Pushing through the brush, tearing through the hanging vines. Now that I wasn't running anymore, the pain—that spiky torture suit of pain—seemed to close over my body again. I ached and burned. Branches scratched my face and arms. Vines and tangled bushes wrapped themselves around my legs like hands trying to hold onto me. I yanked myself free of them. I shoved myself on. With every step, my thirst got worse. I got dizzier. The weakness at my center spread steadily into my legs and arms.

Then, suddenly, I was down. I didn't even remember falling. All at once, I was just lying on the forest floor with my face in the dirt and half my body caught in a tangle of thorny underbrush. I lay there, gasping, barely conscious at all. I tried to listen for voices, for footsteps, for gunfire—to hear if the guards were closing in on me. All I could hear, though, was the harsh, rasping sound of my own breathing and the hammering rhythm of the pulse in the side of my head.

It was a long while before I stopped gasping and another long while before my breathing and heartbeat slowed. Then, as I lay there listening for any sound of the approaching guards, other noises came to me, the noises of the forest. They sort of rose up around me so that I knew they had been there all along and I was just becoming conscious of them. There was a steady flow of birdsong, birds calling to birds in the high trees. There was a steady trill of crickets and the rising, falling rattle of the cicadas. Bees hummed and twigs and dead leaves crackled as the lizards scrambled over them.

I lay there and listened. They were good noises somehow. They were cheerful, peaceful. Exhausted as I was, thirsty beyond belief and scared beyond telling, the noises soothed me. They gave me a sort of lazy, dreamy sensation, and I started to think there might still be some hope—I might still get away from this insanity and back to the life I knew. Maybe someone would find me here, I thought sleepily. Or maybe I would somehow summon enough strength to get up and stumble on a few more steps and find a village or a highway or hikers—or better yet, hunters with guns who would protect me. Or maybe I would just fall asleep and wake up in my own bed, as I had fallen asleep in my bed and woken up in this insanity.

I lay there lazily and listened to the forest noises—birdsong, crickets, bees. And without thinking much, I kind of gazed at my hand, the hand lying on the ground right in front of my eyes. *That's strange*, I thought in a distant, dreamy sort of way. *Where's Beth's number?* Because this was the hand that Beth had written on with her marker yesterday. And though it was bruised and bloody and there was an ugly burn mark on it, I could still see: the number was gone. There wasn't a trace of it. Which really was strange, wasn't it? I remembered how, just before I went to sleep last night, the last thing I did before I turned off the light was to look at my hand and see the number was still there. It was strange—strange that there should be no sign of it now at all.

I lay there gazing at my hand and thinking about that and listening to the forest. My mind drifted from thought to thought, and not all my thoughts made sense as my consciousness came and faded. I don't know how much time passed like that, but the next thing I knew, amid all the birdsong and so on, I became aware of something else: a deep, loud, almost comical burp of a noise. A frog. A big one, by the sound of it. A big old bullfrog honking it up not very far away.

The frog burped again, and it made me smile—it's true—a hunted guy lying there with my face in the dirt and my arm tangled up in scratching branches, and I smiled at the noise the frog made . . . and then I stopped smiling, because an idea had come to me.

I listened harder. Or that is, I shifted the way I was listening. I started listening for noises of a different tone, a different kind. Now, instead of the birdsong and all the rest, I was listening to the sound of the air moving through the treetops. I was hearing the creak and pop of wood bending as the trees stirred this way and that. I heard the low rustle of silence, and finally—there!—there it was—almost buried in that range of sounds but just audible: I heard the trickling whisper of running water.

The frog gave another great big burpy croak, and I not only smiled again, I almost laughed out loud. It was as if he were talking to me, calling to me through the forest, saying, *"Here I am—burp—a frog—burp—and what do frogs like?—burrap!—pardon me; must've been something I ate—they like water!"*

I'm not sure anything else could've gotten me moving again, not even Winston Churchill. But water—oh yeah, I'd move for that. I ran my tongue around my mouth, trying to dampen the terrible dryness there. I braced my hand against the dirt. I started to push myself up. The bushes—those thorns I was lying in—they seemed to grab hold of me, as if they were trying to keep me there, as if they were saying, *Not so fast, Harley-Charlie. What's your hurry, dude? Take it easy. You don't need water! You just need to lie here and sleep, sleep, sleep!*

I gave a growl of resistance. I felt the branches dig into my flesh as I wrestled my arm free of them. Then I was up. On my knees; on my feet. I stood where I was, weak, hunched over, swaying slightly. Listening to the sound of water. Trying to figure out where it was coming from.

The frog croaked again. That was no help. You can't find a frog by the sound of it. Try it sometime. It always sounds like it's coming from where it's not. Every time you move toward it, it comes again from somewhere else.

But the water—I could still hear that. I began to move toward it. Stumbling over the thick jumble of roots and bushes at my feet. Staggering from tree to tree. Leaning against the sturdy trunks to rest and catch my breath again.

The water sound grew louder quickly. In another few moments, I had found it: a small stream. It wound quickly through dead leaves. Its water winked and sparkled beneath the single pale yellow beam of sunlight that fell to the forest floor through the clustered branches above.

I stumbled to it, openmouthed. Dropped to my knees at the edge of it. I fell forward, my mouth seeking out the cool flow.

I didn't know much about forest survival or anything like that, but I knew I was supposed to be careful about drinking water. I remembered something about trying to find the place where the water moved quickest and how you were supposed to be careful not to drink too much or too fast.

Yeah, I remembered all that—but I didn't care. I was just too thirsty. I stuck my mouth on that stream and tried to suck the entire thing right out of the ground in a single gulp. When that wasn't enough, I grabbed handfuls of it and shoveled it into my face as fast as I could.

Oh, it was an amazing sensation. With every gulp, I could feel the strength flowing back into my body. That cloud of dizziness that had closed around my mind—I could feel it breaking up into wisps and drifting away, leaving my thoughts clear. Everything around me—the leaves, the sunlight, the water, the whole world—was suddenly in sharper focus. It was practically magical, like stories from the Bible where people are healed, going from sick to well in a single second.

I drank and drank, and when I couldn't drink anymore, I rolled over on my back and just lay there, gasping and feeling good and strong. I could think clearly again too. With the water in me, with strength in me, I could begin to think and plan, trying to figure out what had happened to me, what I was dealing with, how I could get away and get back home. There had to be a solution to this craziness, after all. There had to be some sort of reasonable explanation. This wasn't a show on the Sci Fi Channel. Those weren't space aliens coming after me. They didn't tractor-beam me out of my bed into another dimension. Somehow I'd just been . . . *stolen* . . . stolen out of my life and shoved into this one. There had to be a method, a reason. And there had to be a way out. There had to be.

But before I could find the answers, I had to start moving again. I had to find my way to a road, to a town, to the police.

I had an idea. I turned over on my side and lifted off the ground—which wasn't easy, believe me. Every time I stopped moving, the stiffness and pain settled over my body again. But with a lot of grunting and groaning, I managed it. I turned over and lifted myself up, and then grabbed hold of the slim trunk of a birch tree and pulled myself to my feet.

I looked down at the water. It had to run somewhere, didn't it? It was just a narrow stream, but still, it had to make its way somewhere. Maybe it just petered out, but maybe it flowed into a bigger river that would lead me, in turn, to a town. Or maybe it ended at a lake, where there'd be vacation homes and boats and phones . . .

I tried to follow the flow with my eyes, to see where the stream led, but it was no good. The stream wound into the trees and disappeared from view. So—weary as I was—I started moving again. I began to follow the bubbling flow of the water.

I stuck close to the stream where the brush was thinnest. I pushed through the trees. I went around the bend.

And my heart sank as I saw where the stream ended.

I saw the water curve around once, and then curve back. Then it came into a clearing, and there . . . it vanished into the earth.

I stood where I was. I stared unhappily at the place where the water disappeared. It was a clearing, an opening in the trees. At the center of it, there was a sort of depression in the earth. It looked almost as if the ground had collapsed there and fallen in on itself. At the bottom of the depression, there was a dark hole, an opening about as big around as a man. It seemed to lead into nothingness, complete blackness. The stream poured out of the deep forest shadows, skipped merrily over the brighter clearing, and then, with the suddenness of a snapped finger, it was gone, through that hole, into that impenetrable dark.

I knew what it was. As I said, I wasn't a big forest survival guy, but I'd hiked in the woods around my home enough and I'd seen this sort of thing before. It was a sinkhole. The stone beneath the dirt here must be soft—limestone maybe. The water had worn a hole in it and there was probably a cave—even a network of caves—underneath.

Well, so much for that idea. There was no way I was going underground into absolute blackness. If I was going to die, I was going to die up here in the light. I'd have to find another way.

I turned from the sinkhole and scanned the forest. It was the same in every direction, the same tangle of branches and vines, the same streaking sunlight, and the same shadows slowly getting deeper, darker. Soon it would be night and there'd be no chance of finding my way. For now, at least I knew I'd been heading in the direction of the sinking sun when I left the compound. If I kept traveling that way, at least I'd put some more distance between me and the bad guys before dusk.

I was just about to set off when I heard it. An unmistakable sound. An engine—*Maybe a car*, I thought with faint hope—but no—no—it was a truck. It was getting louder, coming closer somewhere beyond the trees. It was out on the trail, out of my sightline, but not that far away, not far enough. For another second or two, I tried to hold on to the desperate hope that it was someone besides the guards, someone who might help me.

Then the truck stopped and I heard their voices, and my hope was gone.

"There," one of them said in a thick, syrupy accent. "Look. The branches."

"I see it," said another.

It was the guards all right. They must've had a second truck back in the compound. Or maybe they'd gotten another set of keys to the truck I'd stolen. Or maybe . . . well, it didn't matter, did it? They were here. They were close.

"Looks like he went off that way," said the first man now.

"Yes," said the second. "I see it."

"Dylan and I'll keep watch on the path in case he tries to double back and make a break. You three, take Hunter. Stay in radio contact."

"Will do."

For another second, I stood in the little clearing, unable to think, unable to move. My eyes darted frantically back and forth, looking for a way out—any way. If I was quick, I thought, I still might stay ahead of them, find a place to hide.

But the next moment, I heard something else, something new. It was a sound that seemed to go through me like a dentist's drill hitting a raw nerve.

Take Hunter, the man had said.

And when I heard that next sound, I knew who Hunter was. He was a dog. A bloodhound.

And judging by the long, hungry howl that now came winding to me through the tangled branches, he had found my scent.

He was after me.

CHAPTER TWELVE

Into the Dark

The forest seemed suddenly alive with noise—with noise and danger. The dog howled. The men shouted. Branches and leaves snapped and crackled as they stormed quickly through the underbrush. I couldn't see them yet, but I could tell that they were on my trail. Every moment that passed brought them closer to me.

For another second, I stood where I was, too confused and frightened to move. One more time, my eyes scanned the forest, looking for an escape route. There was none.

Without thinking, I let my hand flutter down to my waistband. I felt the butt of the pistol there, the gun I'd taken from the truck driver. But what good was a pistol against machine guns?

It was no use. No use to run. No use to stand and fight. There was only one thing for me to do.

I turned to face the sinkhole, that opening into absolute blackness. On TV and in the movies and stuff, all you have to do to throw a dog off your trail is splash around in some water. But that's not real. In real life, a dog can follow you through water just fine—I saw it once on the Discovery Channel. But maybe if I went into the caves—maybe I could lose the bloodhound in there . . .

Still, I hesitated. If I went down there and there was nothing, just a dead end, a small chamber, the guards would climb down after me. They would corner me down there and put an end to it. And even if there was a passage, a network of caves, how could I find my way through it? I could be lost forever underground. I could starve to death in the terror of that darkness.

The dog howled. The men shouted. The branches and leaves snapped and crackled. Closer.

"This way!"

"There—over there!"

"The dog's got his scent! Go, go!"

Closer still.

I took a deep, trembling breath. I stepped into the little stream. Splashing through it, I walked unsteadily over the clearing to the sinkhole.

The hole was small, set into the bottom of the depression just like a drain at the bottom of a sink. When I reached it, I had to lie down in order to slide into it feet-first. I lowered myself into the water and mud and mulch that had washed to the mouth of the hole with the current. I eased my feet into the opening, into the unseen.

The hole was narrow. I had to work my way in, turning to lie almost facedown in the muck. I slid my way down the funneling stream and felt my feet go over the edge and into thin air. I gripped the wet, slippery ground to keep from falling. My feet felt around for a ledge I could stand on, for anything I could stand on. There was nothing there. For all I knew, it was a straight drop into oblivion.

Suddenly, the dog let out a fresh howl, so close it felt as if he were standing right beside me, howling into my ear. The men answered him with a fresh round of shouts.

"Here. Look here!"

"Water!"

"Look at the branches."

"He must've found the stream."

"There's the trail!"

"He's following the water!"

"Go, Hunter! Good boy!"

"This way!"

And the branches started crashing again, and the whisk and rattle of the leaves was so near it made the breath catch in my throat. I looked in the direction of the noise. There they were. I caught my first glimpse of them. Hulking shapes moving between the tree trunks. They would be here in a minute, maybe less.

With a grunt of effort, I slid myself farther into the sinkhole. The water and mud now oozed up over my shirt, over my neck. I felt the cold, damp, gritty mud lapping against my cheek, leaking into my mouth. I felt the gun in my waistband press into my belly as my waist went over the edge and the narrow hole closed in around me. I felt my legs kicking, searching for a place to rest, dangling in nothingness. I whispered the fastest prayer I know, probably the oldest prayer known to man: *Help me!*

Then, my fingers clawing at the wet earth, I slid in the rest of the way.

I gripped the edge of the earth as my body hung

down, as I swung my legs against the wall and my feet scrabbled against its slippery surface. Another burst of howling from the dog made me look up. The daylight had telescoped to a narrow gray circle over my head. When I looked down I saw that gray light fade away to nothing.

Finally, I felt something: a little ledge in the rock. I wedged my toes on top of it. But the second I tried to shift my hands from the wet ground above and find a grip on the wall, I slipped. The next moment, I was plunging downward into darkness.

It was a short fall. I landed hard, banging against the wall as I touched down, scraping my knee, tearing my pants. I stumbled, grabbing the wound, grimacing against the pain, trying to keep hold of the slick stone.

I steadied myself. I looked up. The sinkhole was now nothing but a patch of blue sky about as big around as a basketball. The wild howls of the dog and the deep shouts of the guards filtered down through it, fading into echoes.

I looked down. There was just enough light from above to make out where I was standing. I was on a broad ledge of rock with the water from the stream spilling down to it, running over it. My eyes followed that flow to a wall of rock, only just visible, a few feet in front of me. A dead end . . . No, wait: the water ran to the base of that wall and then into a gap at the bottom of it. The gap was long and maybe two feet high. If I laid myself down on the ledge, I should be able to slip into it, slide myself into the space beneath the wall. It wasn't a very nice thought. It'd be a tight fit with no way out. If they caught me in there, there'd be no escape. But what else could I do? I could hear the footsteps of the guards now, crunching over dead leaves, splashing through water. They had come into the clearing. They were right above my head.

I lowered myself onto the cold gray stone. I felt the thin stream of water running into me, bubbling against me, soaking my shirt. With a grunt, I began to shove myself into the gap beneath the wall.

And oh yes, it was tight in there—way tight. I felt as if I were being buried alive, as if the weight of the whole Earth were settling onto my back, pressing down on me. I felt the pistol jammed hard against my belly. There was no room to bring my hand to it, no way I could use it or pull it free. I couldn't even turn my head, couldn't look back to see the sinkhole anymore or the little circle of sky. I could make out only the faintest gray shading in the darkness, the last trace of the light.

Still, I edged in farther underneath the stone. It was like climbing into my own coffin.

It took the guards about ten more seconds to find the sinkhole. Then the sound of their voices changed. They got louder, deeper, more echoic. The dog, Hunter, stopped his howling and let out a series of wild, throaty, triumphant barks. They were right above me. They were looking into the cave.

"Must've gone in here!"

"Well, that's it. He's cornered now!"

"Hey!" the first guard shouted down to me. "West! Come out of there, you're finished."

"Give up, kid. Don't make this worse than it has to be."

How much worse can it get? I thought. I lay there, like a corpse in a coffin, but alive, claustrophobic, trying to keep my breathing steady, trying to keep the panic sparking in my stomach from catching fire and flaming through me.

Another man—another man with a thick accent—cursed. "I can't believe it!"

"We're gonna have to go in after him."

"I can't believe it," the man with the accent said again.

"All right, I'll go. Hold on to the dog. Stupid punk," he muttered—that was referring to me, I guess.

I thought I saw something. I thought the nature of the faint gray light changed. It grew slightly brighter for a moment, then faded again. A flashlight, I thought. One of them was shining a flashlight into the sinkhole.

I heard another curse. The guy must've had his head right down into the sinkhole now. I could even hear him sigh—and even his sigh echoed.

"All right, hold the flashlight right like that so I can see my way," he said. "I'll go down and have a look around."

Instinctively, I shoved myself even farther underneath the rock—and to my immense relief I felt cool, damp air on the fingertips of my right hand. I pushed my hand up and wiggled my fingers. There was nothing above them. There was a way out from underneath the wall. The gap went straight through. There was another opening, up where my hand was, above my head. If I could edge up a little, I might be able to fit through it. It was worth a try anyway, better than getting caught in here.

Above and behind me, the dog let out a series of frantic barks. I could hear the scraping and grunting and cursing—a lot of cursing—as the one guard started his climb down into the sinkhole after me. With the flashlight to guide him, he'd be down in a second. Then all he'd have to do was follow the path of the water like I did. He'd lie down on the rock and see me under there. Then, if I refused to come out, he'd just poke in the muzzle of his AK-47 and blow me to kingdom come.

So I had to move—now. Crawling on my belly, I inched my way under the wall, toward the opening. I was moving away from the sinkhole light and the flashlight light too. The darkness closed over me like a steel trap until I couldn't see a thing—not a thing—it was absolute, pitch black. I squirmed up farther along the narrow passage. My arm was free of the wall. Then my head popped out into that dank air. Then I got my shoulder out. Clawed my way over the stone, pulling my legs after me into the open.

Then I was free. I let out a gasping breath of relief. I turned over.

And I fell off the edge of rock.

The next moment I was rolling down and down and down. Bouncing hard off the stone, feeling it scrape pieces of flesh away from my face and arms. I couldn't see. I was completely blind. There was nothing but motion and rock and pain, and I had no idea whether I was about to plunge off another edge and just drop straight down . . .

But no. No, I hit bottom. I felt the jar of the impact go through my entire body so that my bones ached. The breath was knocked out of me in a loud grunt. I lay stunned in a darkness so complete that when I lifted my hand in front of me, I literally could not see my fingers an inch in front of my eyes.

I lay still, aching, gasping for breath, staring up at nothingness.

Then the nothingness was broken. The pale, pale out-glow of a flashlight's beam appeared overhead for a single moment, then was gone. It was the guard. Obviously, he was lying down, poking his flashlight into the gap in the wall, looking for me.

I held my breath, watching as the dim glow appeared again, then faded.

Then the guard shouted, "He's not here!"

He couldn't see the opening I'd fallen through. It was out of his sightline.

The shout came back to him from above. "What do you mean he's not there! Listen to this dog. He's going crazy!"

As if in agreement, Hunter the dog sent up a fresh chorus of ferocious barking.

"I'm telling you," shouted the guard above me, "there's nothing down here. There's nowhere for him to hide! Idiot dog must be after a squirrel or something."

He sighed again. Cursed again. The next time he spoke, his voice sounded farther away. "Throw me a rope, man. This place is giving me the creeps. Probably bats down here and everything."

I heard him grunt again and go through another long series of curses as he retreated, as he climbed back up the wall, back through the sinkhole into the upper world. I heard his voice again as he reached the top.

"Let's get out of here."

I heard his footsteps receding. The dog's wild and argumentative barks grew dimmer as the men dragged him away from the sinkhole.

Finally, silence. I couldn't hear any of them anymore.

Still, I didn't move. I lay a long time in the absolute darkness, absolutely still. Trying to think. Trying to make sense out of what was happening to me. Looking for an answer.

CHAPTER THIRTEEN

Sensei Mike

What happened next? I asked myself. After the karate demonstration in school, I mean. After Beth came to the cafeteria and wrote her number on my hand. What happened after that? There was nothing. Nothing special, I mean. Nothing I could remember, anyway.

It was just a day. Just an ordinary day.

The truth is, after that talk with Beth, I guess I got a little blissed out, a little—how can I put it?—goofy. I remember going from class to class, doing my work and everything. But I don't remember too many of the details. I guess it was mostly me sitting in my seat, sort of looking at my hand, sort of turning my hand this way and that, admiring the phone number written on it. Goofy, like I said.

After school, I went home for a while and did some homework. Then, just like every other Wednesday, I took my mom's car—the Ford Explorer—and drove out to the Eastfield Mall for my karate lesson with Sensei Mike.

The karate school isn't much to look at. It's just a small storefront in the mall. There's a sign over the window that says KARATE STUDIO in black letters. That's the only name it has.

It's a simple set-up inside too. There's a small anteroom where you come in and take off your shoes—there are no shoes allowed in the *dojo* itself. There's a small office next to the anteroom with a desk and a computer and a phone and all that. And there's the dojo—an open carpeted space for practicing—with a punching bag hanging in one corner, a big American flag hanging on one wall, and a wall of mirrors opposite that. Also, wherever there's space, there's a lot of cool swords and axes and other weapons hanging on pegs.

Sensei Mike owned the place and ran it. There were three or four other teachers who worked there, but Sensei Mike was the best. He was the coolest too. In fact, Sensei

Mike was probably the coolest person I knew. He was—I don't know—maybe thirty-five years old or something. He stood about six feet tall, slim but with broad shoulders. He had a lot of neatly combed black hair that always seemed to stay in place even when he was sparring or working out. His face was long and lean, with a lot of lines chiseled into it. He had a mustache, a real big soup-strainer that hung down over the sides of his mouth. Under the mustache, you could see there was always a sort of smile playing at the corners of his lips. The smile was in his brown eyes too. He always seemed to be laughing about something to himself.

Sensei Mike had been in the Army for a long time. He'd been in the War against Terror, fighting against the Islamic extremists both in Afghanistan and in Iraq.

"I'd still be over there," he liked to tell us, "but I had to come back and knock some sense into all you chuckleheads."

Actually, the truth was more complicated than that. I knew this because I looked Mike up on the Internet once and found some news stories about him. The truth was: Mike came home because he was wounded in action and had to have a piece of titanium put in his leg. The news stories said he'd been working with a task force that was helping to build a school in Afghanistan. The task force came under attack by more than a hundred Taliban fighters. Mike had to battle his way to a big .50-caliber machine gun that was mounted on an armored truck. He was wounded and surrounded by the enemy on three sides, but he used the big gun to hold them off, and the task force was saved. The president gave him a medal for it and everything—I mean, the actual president, as in the President of the United States. It was a pretty cool story. I couldn't get Mike to talk about it, though. I tried to once. I asked him about it, but he just shrugged and said, "There's not a soldier out there who wouldn't do what I did and better. I just happened to be the first chuckle-head to get to the gun."

Mike was the teacher on duty that Wednesday. After some warm-up exercises and some katas, he set me to sparring with Lou Wilson. Now, the main thing you have to understand about Lou is that Lou is big. Very big. Not very tall or anything, just about my height, but broad and thick and heavy and strong. If I had to compare him to something, it'd probably be a cement mixer. When you're sparring with Lou and he comes at you, it's like standing in the middle of the road while a cement mixer comes barreling your way.

That said, I'd always had good luck sparring with Lou. I generally got the better of the fight. Lou is a really nice guy, really friendly and all, but, just being honest here, you'd have to say he's not all that strong in the brains department. Doesn't have a lot of smarts, not in school and not when it comes to fighting. He comes at you like a cement mixer all right—and you dance out of his way and pepper him with punches and kicks. And then he comes at you like a cement mixer again and you do the same thing again. And that's pretty much the way our sparring usually goes.

Only not today.

Now, we always try to do things safely in the dojo, and sparring's no different. We wear soft gloves and a helmet and shin pads and, of course, a hard cup for protection. Sure, you can get bruised ribs or a fat lip on a bad day, but in general, no one's going to hurt you too much.

The one exception to that rule would be if you were to—oh, let's just say for example—get run over by a cement mixer. Which I was. Or at least it felt as if I were.

I'm not sure exactly how it happened. When we started out, it was the usual scenario. There I was in my sparring gear, and there was Lou in his. Sensei Mike

128

stood between us, wearing his black gi and his black belt with four red stripes—a very high ranking. He had Lou and me face each other in the front position. We bowed karate-style to show that we respected each other and that we were working together to learn karate and not trying to do any real damage.

Then Sensei Mike said, "On guard." We both leapt back and put up our fists in fighting position.

Sensei Mike lifted his hand between us. Then he dropped it and said, "Go!"

And, as always, here came Lou the Cement Mixer. Rumble, rumble, rumble. And I did my usual dancing out of the way, peppering him with a couple of good jabs to the side of his helmet and one sharp roundhouse kick into his stomach above his belt. And then here came Lou again, rumble, rumble, rumble. And again, I danced out of the way and hit and kicked him.

Now, mind you, the blows didn't bother Lou any. If you wanted to bother Lou, I really think you'd have to sneak up behind him and hit him with a brick. That might annoy him a little, anyway. As it was, I got to show off my karate style—and Lou just came a-rumbling at me again.

And I remember thinking to myself: *Boy, if Beth could see me now, she would be really impressed.*

Then, right after that, I remember thinking, *I wonder why I'm looking up at the ceiling with stars twinkling in front of my eyes and birds twittering in my ears?*

As nearly as I can reconstruct it, what happened was this:

Once again, Lou came at me, rumble, rumble, rumble. Once again, I was getting ready to dance out of the way. But instead of dancing out of the way, I started thinking about Beth and how impressed she would be if she could see me dancing out of the way. Lou, finding to his delight that instead of being somewhere else I was standing in front of him *thinking* about being somewhere else, decided that this might be a good opportunity to throw a roundhouse right to the side of my head. Which he did. Whereupon I went down on my backside, and cue the twinkling stars and twittering birds.

Of course, I jumped back up to my feet right away—just as soon as I realized I had left them. I didn't want Sensei Mike to think I couldn't take a punch—even if it was a punch from a cement mixer. I started dancing around again immediately with my fists up in front of me, trying to pretend that a chorus of *boings* and *dings* wasn't still going off inside my head.

Luckily, about two seconds after that, Sensei Mike stopped the fight. He laughed and slapped me and Lou both on our shoulders.

"All right, chuckleheads, good job. Salute the flag and go get dressed."

Lou and I punched our gloves together—a way of shaking hands.

"Nice punch," I said. "You really tagged me with that one."

Under his helmet, I could see Lou beam with pride. Then we both turned and gave a karate-style bow to the American flag.

There's a changing room at the back of the dojo, just big enough for one person. I waited for Lou to finish, then I went in and stripped my gi off and climbed back into my street clothes. There's no shower or anything in there, so I don't usually wash up until I get home and my mother gets a whiff of me.

When I was dressed, I walked across the dojo, carrying my karate bag. At the edge of the anteroom, I turned and gave one last bow of respect to the dojo. Then I walked out.

Lou had left already. Mike was sitting in the office behind his computer, typing up some notes.

"Thanks, Sensei," I called in to him.

"Hey, chucklehead," he said without looking up. "Get in here."

I walked in and stood in front of the desk. Sensei Mike finished whatever he was typing. Then he sat back in his chair, put his hands behind his head, and looked up at me.

"How's your gray matter?" he said. "That was a pretty good one Lou got in on you."

"Yeah, it was a good shot, I gotta admit," I said. I didn't sound happy about it, and, in fact, I wasn't. But the truth is the truth. It was a pretty good shot.

"You want to be careful with that head of yours," Sensei Mike said. He hid his smile by bringing one hand around and smoothing his mustache with his thumb and forefinger. "Brains are more important than fists, you know. It's no good learning karate if you get knocked stupid in the process."

I tried to laugh it off. Sometimes you win in sparring and sometimes you lose, and you have to get used to that. But—again, the truth is the truth—I don't much like losing. I don't suppose anyone does. "I just forgot to duck, that's all," I said.

"Sure," said Sensei Mike, still smoothing his 'stache.

"I guess you just got distracted by all your math homework."

I didn't know what he meant. "Math homework?"

"Yeah," said Mike. He swiveled back and forth in his chair, smoothing his mustache, hiding his smile. "You must have a lot of math homework, seeing as you ran out of room in your notebook and had to start writing the numbers on your hand. I guess it was thinking about the numbers on your hand that distracted you."

I looked stupidly down at my hand for a second. Then I got it, and I felt the color rising up into my face.

Sensei Mike laughed. "Don't sweat it, chucklehead. I'm just giving you a hard time."

I rolled my eyes, embarrassed.

"The fact is," said Sensei Mike, "you've been distracted around here a lot lately. I guess I was just wondering: is that all about . . . your math homework?"

I shrugged. "I guess so," I said.

"Nothing else."

I shrugged again. "Well, there's a lot of stuff. You know, school and whatnot."

"You gonna tell me about it or am I gonna have to beat it out of you?"

"Well . . ." I wagged my head back and forth. I didn't

really want to talk to him about it. I didn't want to talk to anyone about it. But before I knew it, I heard myself saying, "There is one thing . . ."

I was sorry the minute the words came out of my mouth. I was sorry, and, weirdly enough, I was kind of happy at the same time. Because there was this one thing on my mind that I'd wanted to bring up to Sensei Mike for a long time. It was this secret ambition I had that I hadn't told anybody. The reason I hadn't told anybody was because I wasn't sure it was possible. If there was anyone who would know, it was Sensei Mike.

Now the thing about Sensei Mike is: he tells you the truth. He's not one of these happy-talk guys who'll say what you want to hear or what he thinks you're supposed to hear because he read it in some article or something. He'll tell you his best opinion, flat out, without mincing words. So I was happy because I wanted to know his opinion. But I was sorry because I was afraid of what his opinion might be.

So I took a deep breath. I went into a side pocket of my karate bag and wrestled out a battered old paperback book I kept hidden there. I'd found it in a box at a fundraising book sale they'd had at the public library. I'd been reading it and reading it in secret for weeks now, cover to cover and back again. I kept it in my karate bag because sometimes my mother goes through my school bag to clean out the half-eaten lunches and so on. But she leaves my karate bag alone. I didn't want her to find it because, like I said before, I knew it would drive her crazy with fear and I'd never hear the end of it. And I knew if I asked my father about it, he'd tell my mother, so I couldn't talk to him either.

I held the book out to Sensei Mike. It was called: *To Be a U.S. Air Force Pilot.*

Sensei Mike took the book in one hand and glanced down at it.

"What do you think?" I said. "You think I could make it as a fighter pilot in the Air Force?"

Sensei Mike pulled the book close to himself. Leaning back in the chair, swiveling back and forth, he opened it, paged through it.

"Cool," he murmured. "Cool jets."

He glanced through a few more pages, then shut the book and held it out to me. I took it and stuffed it back down into my karate bag.

I stood there, nervous, waiting to hear the answer to my question.

"You wanna be an Air Force pilot?" he asked me.

I managed to nod.

"Really tough. Really tough training. Very selective, very elite. A lot of guys don't make it. Even some of the best. Just not that many slots open."

I went on nodding. I already knew all that.

Sensei Mike folded his hands on the knot of his black belt. "You know, a lot of guys, teachers and so on—they'd be happy to tell you that you can be anything you want to be, anything you set your mind on. You go to them, they'll tell you you should feel good about yourself, that you're special and all that stuff."

"I know that, Sensei Mike. That's why I didn't go to them. I asked you 'cause I want the truth."

"The truth is: you can't be anything you want to be. All that talk is garbage. I mean, I could try till my ears smoked, but I couldn't write a symphony—not a good one, anyway. I couldn't throw a baseball ninety-five miles an hour or hit one out of a major-league park. I want to do all those things, but it doesn't matter how hard I try—I just wasn't given those abilities." Sensei Mike came forward in his chair, leaned forward, and looked up at me hard. "But this is also the truth: if you try your best and better than your best, and work and push yourself until you think you can't go on and then push yourself some more—then—then if you have a little bit of luck on your side—then you can be all the good things God made you to be."

"Well, I'd do that," I said. "You know I would. You've seen me. I'd bust my chops for this."

"Yeah, you would, that's true."

"So what do you think? Could I do it?"

He turned it over in his mind one more second. Then he said, "Absolutely. With your brains, your reflexes, and the way you work . . . assuming you meet the physical requirements, the eyesight and all that . . . I think you got Ace written all over you." He pointed a finger at me. "You'll still be a chucklehead—but you'll be an Ace chucklehead."

"I don't know, Mike," I said. "You gotta get a congressman to nominate you and everything."

"Don't sweat it. I know plenty of congressmen. I know some Air Force brass too. Finish your education, pull down the big grades, and you'll get your shot, I promise you. And hey . . . meanwhile, try to keep your mind on what you're doing. You can't fly jets if Lou Wilson splatters your brains all over the dojo."

When I walked out of the karate studio that day, I felt like I was about ten feet tall, a giant among men looking down at the world from high above. My mind was racing over all kinds of things, over everything that had happened that day. The karate demonstration and the way all the kids shouted and applauded. Beth coming into the cafeteria the way she did, and the way we talked and she wrote on my hand and everything. And now, Sensei Mike: *I think you got Ace written all over you . . .*

I had this feeling—this incredible feeling—that it was actually possible that I could turn my daydreams into reality.

It was just like Sensei Mike said. My mind was totally in the clouds. I wasn't paying attention. I was completely unprepared for what happened next.

It was getting toward evening now, around five o'clock or so. On the far side of the mall, in the gap between the Pizza Kitchen and the movie theater— beyond where the movie theater parking was—I could see the sun turning red as it reached the tops of the far hills. I took a deep breath of the cool September air. I wished I could get in my mom's car and drive out to those hills and look out from the top of them toward the setting sun and see my future out there—see what was going to happen and what it would be like, and end all the suspense I felt inside me.

I guess it's a good thing I couldn't do that. If I had seen what my future was really going to be like, I would've gone home that night and hidden under the bed.

Anyway, I had to get back for dinner. Plus I still had my history paper to write.

So I started walking across the parking lot. I'd parked the car in back of Paulson's, the mall supermarket. That part of the lot wasn't the nicest place in the mall. It was where the garbage Dumpsters were. It was also where the homeless guys hung out—the crazy ones and the alcoholic ones who pawed through the Dumpsters for food. Kids hung out there sometimes too. Everyone knew there were some checkout people in Paulson's who would sell you beer without checking your ID. So sometimes kids bought a beer in Paulson's and drank it in the back by the Dumpsters after the police patrols had passed through.

What I mean is: that rear area wasn't a great place to be, especially after dark. But on a busy day like today, when the parking lot was practically full, it was easier to find a space back there because the shopping moms avoided it. Anyway, I knew I'd be out of karate before dark, and I wasn't worried. I went down the narrow lane next to Paulson's and came around the back. I reached my car. Opened the hatch. Threw in my karate bag.

Then I stopped. Stopped with my hand on the hatch door, about to push it down.

I had lifted my eyes to scan the area, make sure nothing threatening was going on. As I was turning away, I spotted a group of kids slouching against a brick wall near the Dumpsters. There were three of them. They all had paper bags in their hands. They were lifting the paper bags to their mouths and lowering them again. I knew there were beer bottles in the bags.

One of the kids was Alex Hauser. He was glaring at me. He lifted his paper bag to his lips and lowered it again. I waved to him. He didn't smile or wave back. He just tapped one of his friends on the shoulder. He pointed me out to him.

With that, the three kids pushed their way off the wall. They tossed their paper bags into one of the Dumpsters. They started coming my way, with Alex in the lead.

They didn't look friendly.

CHAPTER FOURTEEN

Alex

Alex had changed a lot since our best-friend days. He almost looked like a different person now. He used to be a kind of happy, open-faced, round-faced guy, but now his face looked narrow and hungry; sullen too. His mouth was set in a permanent frown, like the mouths of those bass I caught in Lake Wyatt sometimes. His eyes seemed to flash with anger. He was wearing a watch cap and a blue tracksuit. His two friends were also in tracksuits. One, a dark-skinned guy, had a red bandana on. The other had his blond hair cut to the nub. I guessed they were from Alex's new school. I didn't know them, anyway. Frankly, I wasn't looking forward to an introduction.

I shut the hatch door as Alex reached me. He stuck out his fist. I touched it with mine by way of hello. Alex smiled with one corner of his mouth. It wasn't a friendly smile, not really. It was that nasty smile guys wear when they're planning to start trouble but they don't want to give you an excuse to say so.

"Hey, Charlie," he said. "How's it working for you?"

"Pretty good, pretty good. How you doing, Alex?"

"Excellent, excellent. Guess you're still doing your karate, huh?" And then suddenly, he let out a loud karate shout and jumped into a sort of mock fighting position. It was meant to startle me, meant to make me jump and look stupid. Which I guess I did a little. Not much, but enough so Alex could laugh at me and the two punks with him could laugh too. "Charlie here is a black belt," Alex said to the others.

The crew-cut guy said, "Pretty tough guy, huh," as if he thought that was funny.

I didn't like the feel of this at all. I hadn't seen Alex in a long time. I could tell he'd changed a lot. But I didn't think he'd do anything crazy like start a fight with me or anything. I mean, why would he?

Then Alex said: "Hey. I heard something funny today."

"Oh yeah?" I said warily.

"Yeah. Really funny. You wanna hear?"

I shrugged. "Sure. What's so funny?"

"It's just a funny rumor I heard about you."

"About me?"

Crew-cut Guy snickered nastily. I was beginning not to like Crew-cut Guy.

"About me?" Alex echoed. He made a face—a sort of stupid face to suggest I was acting stupid, pretending not to know something I really did know. "Yeah," he said then in a friendly voice that was not very friendly, "about you," and he poked me in the shoulder hard enough so it hurt. I stared at him. It really was as if he was a totally different person. Not the Alex I knew at all. "I heard a story about you that was really hilarious. That you were going out with Beth Summers."

I felt something inside me then. It was like an icy hand had taken hold of a piece of me and twisted it. Was it possible Alex had been waiting for me out here? He probably knew when my karate lesson was. I hadn't changed my schedule in years. Was it possible he'd brought his friends here so he could confront me about Beth? Could he have already heard about my conversation with her in the cafeteria? Sure he could. Alex still knew people in my school. They could've seen me with Beth and called him. Had it made him angry enough to come out here with a couple of punks to try to start a fight with me?

"Is that right?" he said. "You going out with Beth?"

"I don't know," I told him. "I might sometime, maybe. Why? You have a problem with that?"

Alex made an elaborate gesture of indifference. "No. I don't have a problem with that. Why would I have a problem? Hey—" He gave an ugly laugh and sort of backhanded my shoulder in the same spot where he'd poked me. "Hey, I hope you get more out of her than I did. I mean, she's kind of an uptight little stick, if you ask me."

Now the Bible says you're not supposed to keep anger in your heart, and I hoped I wouldn't keep it, but it was there now, all right. In fact, so much anger flared up in me when he said that about Beth that I almost felt my fist was going to shoot up and knock Alex across the parking lot before I could stop it. But I did stop it. You can't hit a guy for what he says, even if it stinks. So I just answered him—quietly, you know—working hard to keep my voice steady.

"Well," I said, "I guess I didn't ask you, did I? And now I'm going home."

I started to move away. Crew-cut Guy reached out to grab me. The way I was feeling just then, this was not a good idea on the part of Crew-cut Guy.

"Hey, where you going . . . ?" he said—or started to say. Because before he could finish, I took a step back away from him, turning as I did. At the same time, I put my hands up on guard. I didn't exactly slap his hand away. I just sort of gently deflected it with the back of my hand at the same time I slipped out of his reach. Crew-cut Guy's grabbing fingers went right past me and caught hold of nothing but empty air.

It was a good move. With that one turning step I'd maneuvered myself past all three of them. I'd gotten away from the back of the Explorer so they couldn't corner me against it.

I lowered my hands now. I didn't want them up in fighting position. I didn't want to provoke Crew-cut Guy to take a swing at me because if he did, I might have to hurt him, and I didn't want to hurt him—well, all right, I did want to hurt him, but I wasn't going to. Anyway, I could get my hands up fast enough if I needed them.

"You guys have a good night," I said quietly.

For a second it looked like Crew-cut Guy was going to come after me. The anger was raging in his eyes, and he made a move. But Alex held him back, pressing the back of his hand against his chest. He was looking at me, Alex was, and kind of half-smiling, a strange smile, almost as if he admired me.

"Don't be stupid," he told Crew-cut Guy, holding him there without taking his eyes off me. "He'd put you in the hospital."

I could see Crew-cut Guy was angry about that, but he held back. I was grateful to Alex for stopping him. I saluted him with one finger to my head.

"Why don't you give me a call sometime?" I said. "We could talk. Privately."

I walked around the side of the car. I yanked the driver's door open while Alex's two friends glared at me. I slid in behind the wheel and shut the door.

The anger was still hot in me. In fact, it was worse now—now that I was away from them and didn't have to worry about doing something violent and stupid. Now the anger closed my throat and made my stomach clutch. It was a rotten feeling.

I jammed my key into the ignition and twisted it

hard, turning the engine over. I grabbed hold of the gear-shift, ready to throw the big car into reverse.

Just then, the passenger door opened and Alex slid into the seat beside me.

"All right," he said. "You wanna talk? Let's talk. Drive somewhere."

CHAPTER FIFTEEN

Argument

With Alex in the car beside me, I drove out of the parking lot, the Explorer's tires bouncing hard over the exit ramp and out onto the road. I guess—being as angry as I was—I was driving a little too fast. I had to ease down on the brake, bring the big car under control—and bring myself under control too. I took a deep breath and forced myself to loosen my jaw, which was clenched together like a bear trap.

Alex didn't say anything as I drove out over Route

109, past the other big mall in town. The silence hung there between us. I was the one who broke it.

"I like your friends," I said. Only the way I said it, it meant the opposite.

"They're okay."

"Oh yeah, they're great. The kind of guys who'll always be around when you need them."

"Hey, they're my friends, all right?"

That almost set me off. I almost started yelling at him right then and there: about Beth, about the punks he hung out with, about everything. But somehow I managed to swallow it all and keep my mouth shut. I mean, Alex had gotten into the car. He wanted to talk to me. That had to be a good sign, right? It wouldn't do any good if I just got on his case.

"Yeah, fine," was all I said finally.

Alex jammed a hand into his tracksuit pocket. He brought out a pack of cigarettes.

"Hey, look . . ." I said.

"Oh, what?" he snapped back. "Are you my mother now or something?"

"It's my mom's car, all right? No smoking. You want a cigarette, we'll park somewhere, you can shove the whole pack in your mouth and set your face on fire for all I care."

There was more silence as Alex reluctantly stuffed the cigarettes back in his tracksuit. Then, a second later, I heard him give kind of a snort. The sound surprised me. I glanced over at him. Unbelievably, he was cracking up: laughing, laughing hard, his smile broad and happy just like it used to be back in the days when we hung out together.

He shook his head, wiping his eyes, laughing. "'Set your face on fire,'" he said. "You are such an idiot."

I had to laugh at that too. "It does make a pretty funny picture . . ."

"Whoosh!" he said, imitating the noise his face might make if it went up in flames.

That made me laugh some more.

After a while, our laughter died away. I turned the car off the big road and headed down Oak Street. It's a nice long quiet lane of houses set back behind rows of trees. The trees' branches form a canopy over the road. It made it pretty dark with the sun so low and the yellowing September leaves shading the pavement. I turned the headlights on. We drove another few seconds without talking.

"Listen," I said, "if you don't want me to ask Beth out . . ."

I left that hanging there, hoping he'd tell me to forget the whole thing. But he didn't. He said, "Yeah? What then? What if I don't want you to ask Beth out?"

"Well," I said, "I'll probably ask her out anyway. But I'll feel bad about it for a few minutes, if that'll help you any."

I heard Alex let out a long breath next to me. "Nah," he said. "Why shouldn't you go out with her? She's not going out with me. In fact, you guys'd probably have a good time together. I mean, she's the coolest girl I ever met." I felt him glance at me as I drove. "That stuff I said about her back at the mall: that was just me mouthing off. I didn't mean it."

That passed for an apology as far as I was concerned, and it was good to hear—really good. It made the anger go out of my heart completely. And let me tell you, it was nice to get rid of it.

"Things are just tough right now," Alex said in a soft voice.

"Sure, I get it," I said. I was glad I was driving. Glad it was getting dark. Glad Alex and I didn't have to look at each other and could just talk. "You mean with your folks and everything."

"Yeah," said Alex. "It's the 'everything' that gets you."

"What do you mean?"

He was quiet a long time. The shadows of the trees passed steadily over the windshield. Behind the trees, the lights of houses began to come on, yellow and warm in the deepening evening. The lights made you think of good things: people having dinner together or watching some show on TV and laughing together. That's what they made me think of, anyway.

"Aw, nothing," Alex said then. "You wouldn't get it."

"Get what?"

"The whole thing. It's like . . . forget it." There was anger in his voice—anger and a kind of weariness.

"Well, try me," I told him. "I mean, whatever it is, I can't get it if you don't explain it to me."

"It's not that, it's . . . It's you, Charlie. It's the way you are. You think everything's so simple. You know? You walk around all sure of yourself. You think good is good and bad is bad. You think, *Work hard, pray to God, respect your parents, love America, and everything'll be great.*"

"I never said everything'd be great. I just feel better about myself when I try to do what's right, that's all."

"See, that's what I mean. Everything's so straight and narrow for you. It's like you were brainwashed by your parents or something, and now you believe all that

goody-good-guy garbage. Things would look a lot different to you if everything weren't so easy. I mean, nothing's
ever gone bad for you. Not really bad."

It made me feel kind of insulted, him saying that. I
could feel myself getting angry all over again. My first
impulse was to argue with him. To tell him things weren't
easy for me all the time. I wanted to tell him about how
my mom sometimes nagged me to death and my sister
drove me crazy and my dad worked too much and how
sometimes I worried about . . . oh, all kinds of stuff, a lot
of stuff. Sometimes things weren't easy at all.

Luckily, though, I managed to pull off my now-famous
keep-the-old-mouth-shut routine yet again. I had to eat
my pride to do it this time, but I figured if I started arguing about me, then we'd never get around to talking about
him. And I figured, the way things were going in his life,
it was probably more important for us to talk about him.

So I just said, "Okay," and waited, driving under the
trees and past the warm lights of the houses.

It worked. Alex went on, talking faster now, as if the
words were just pouring out of him almost before he
could think of them. "I mean, it's easy to believe in things
when everything's going right, when you go home and
your folks are there, and you don't have to worry about

where you're gonna live or what you're gonna eat or anything. Then it's easy to say, *Oh, work hard and pray to God and everything'll be great. In this wonderful free country of ours, blah, blah, blah.* But, I mean, what if all that stuff's a lie, Charlie? You ever consider that? I mean, what if you come home one day and your dad's gone—I mean, just gone, like he never even existed—or like being your dad didn't mean anything to him? And you gotta listen to your mother crying in her bedroom all the time because she's alone and she doesn't have enough money and you don't even know whether you're gonna be able to stay in your crummy house. What good is working hard then, Charlie? What good is 'America the Beautiful'? And where's God—what's he doing about it?"

"He's still there, Alex," I said quietly. "He's right with you the whole way."

"Oh, thanks a lot!" he snapped angrily. "What good does that do me? Huh? I mean, don't you ever ask yourself: what if it's all a lie? I have. Not just me either. A lot of people."

"What do you mean? What's all a lie?"

"Everything!" Alex was really worked up now. I could see him out of the corner of my eye, waving his hands around as he talked. "I mean, they tell you God is

154

good and they tell you America is good and they tell you this is the way to live, free like this where you can do whatever you want . . . but what if that's not true? What if none of it's true? I mean, my dad did whatever he wanted. What's so good about that? I mean, what if we need to tear it all down—all the religious stuff and the patriotism stuff and everything—and just start again in a new way, a stronger way?"

We were coming to the end of Oak Street. There was a park here. Just a small neighborhood place with a ball field and a picnic ground and a couple of tennis courts on the far side. It was empty now, the dark folding down over it. I could see little globes of white light shining where the park's security lamps had come on.

I turned the corner and pulled the Explorer over to the curb. I stopped next to the park and turned the engine off. I could hear the quiet of the night falling outside. Crickets chirping out in the grass and the faint whisper of traffic over on 109.

I turned in my seat and faced Alex. "All right. What are you talking about? I don't understand what you're saying."

Alex's hands moved around as he tried to explain. Even in the growing dark, I could see the pain in his face.

"I'm talking about being lied to! I'm talking about . . . everything you thought was true turning out to be a lie and . . . and about changing everything so it's better!"

"Look, I know things are hard with your folks breaking up, but . . ."

"It's not that! It's not just that. It's not just me, Charlie. There's a lot of people—good people, smart people— who say the same thing."

I shook my head a little, confused. "What people? Who? Who are you talking to?"

"Well . . ." His mouth moved as if he wanted to say more, but no words came out. "Just people, that's all. I mean, you listen to people, right? You're always telling me what your dad says, or what your minister says, or . . . Sensei Mike—man, you never stop talking about him."

"Okay, sure," I said. "I mean, you gotta find people in the world you trust, right? People who know more than you and will tell it to you straight and help you out. What's wrong with that?"

"Nothing! Nothing! That's just what I'm talking about. That's just what I'm saying: maybe I have people in my life who see through all this stuff, you know?"

"All this . . . ?"

"All this rah-rah for God and school and home and

America. Maybe I have people I trust who know better than all that."

I let out a long breath. I ran my hand up through my hair. *Man, poor Alex,* I was thinking. *He is way messed up. Way.*

"All right," I said—trying not to sound like I was arguing with him, keeping my voice really quiet. "Look. I'm not gonna tell you I know what you're going through."

"You don't!"

"You're right," I said. "I don't. And maybe you're even right about things being easy for me. I mean, I've got my problems like everybody, but at least my mom and dad are at home and I'm not worrying about where I'll live and all that . . ."

"Right!" Alex drove his fist down onto his knee. "Right."

"But look at it from the other direction, okay? Maybe with you being upset about things and all . . ."

"I'm not upset," he said, upset.

"All right, all right. But maybe, with the way your life is going right now and the way you're feeling about things—maybe you're not thinking so clearly. You ever consider that? I mean, like, maybe you're so ticked off about everything that you're not picking your friends too well right now. You see what I mean?"

He didn't answer. He sat in the dark looking down at his lap, shaking his head back and forth, shaking and shaking it as if he didn't want to hear me out.

"I mean . . ." I looked around for an example to explain what I was trying to say. "What if you lost a ball game, right? A really big game, you know, so you felt really bad. And you're sitting there on the bench with your head hanging down to your knees, right? And people start coming up to you and saying things like, *What're you playing this stupid game for anyway? Look how bad it makes you feel. Just give it up, man, you know. All that working out and training—you don't need that stuff. You could just go to the mall and have a beer instead. It's just a dumb game anyway, right?* And so on, like that. Those people saying that stuff—would they be your friends, Alex? Would they be your real friends? Or is your friend the coach—you know, like, even big dumb Coach Friedman—who'd come over and say to you, *Hey, I know how tough that was. I been there, but now you gotta work out even more and train even harder and become even better so you're ready to try again.*"

"You don't know what you're talking about." Alex just

went on shaking and shaking his head. His voice was a low growl. "You don't know what you're talking about."

I sighed. "Look—I'm not saying I know. I'm just trying to figure out what makes sense. I mean, your folks broke up—that happens to a lot of people."

"That doesn't make it any better. People keep saying that. That doesn't make it better."

"I know. But here you are, you're feeling really bad, you're feeling down, and I'm asking you: Who're your friends now, Alex? Are they these people who are saying to you, *Hey, things are going bad and you feel bad so you should give up on everything you know is good and true?* Or is your real friend that other voice that's, like, talking inside you . . ."

"Shut up!"

It was like a punch the way he said it. The way he turned to me suddenly with his eyes so bright and furious that they seemed to glow in the dark of the car. It was the tears that made his eyes look like that. The tears in his eyes caught the glow of a streetlamp and reflected it at me.

Alex sneered. "What do you know about what's going on inside me? There's no voice inside me. There's nothing! There's nobody! That's the whole point."

I reached over to give him a friendly punch in the shoulder. "Man . . ."

"No!" He slapped my hand away. "I've had enough of all these . . . lies! *Don't give up! Trust in God! Get up and try again!* What for? Why is it all on me? I didn't do anything. I didn't leave anybody."

"Nobody's blaming you. I'm just saying . . ."

"I know what you're saying! I know what everybody's saying!" He was really yelling now, really loud. A woman walking her dog on the opposite sidewalk actually turned and looked our way—that's how loud he was yelling. "And I'm sick of it! You understand me? You and Beth and my father and everybody! I'm just sick of all of you!"

"Come on, man, chill out . . ."

He shoved me—hard—hit me in the shoulder with his open hand. He let out an ugly curse and pushed the door open. He was so furious it took him three tries to get the handle working, and then he kicked it in a rage. He jumped out of the car. He started stalking away from me into the park.

I climbed out of the driver's seat.

"Hey, Alex, come on . . ."

By the time I came around the hood, he was already

striding across the grass, his figure getting dimmer and dimmer as the darkness of the park closed over him.

"Alex!" I shouted.

I ran a few steps after him into that darkness. I guess he heard me coming because he wheeled around. He pointed his finger at me. "Just stay away from me!" he shouted. "You're not the only one who knows how to fight! Next time I won't be so easy on you!"

Then he turned and started jogging away from me toward the tennis courts.

What could I do? I stood where I was and watched him go.

CHAPTER SIXTEEN

The Cave

I opened my eyes and a jolt of terror shot through me. I couldn't see. Where was I? What was happening?

I had fallen asleep—I had no idea for how long. And when I came to—before I remembered where I was or even who I was—I could see nothing, absolutely nothing. It was as if I had gone blind.

Then I remembered. The torture room. My escape from the compound. The woods. The cave.

I was still in the cave. I had escaped the guards and

fallen deeper underground. That's why I couldn't see, why the darkness around me was so complete.

As soon as it came back to me, the terror I felt was replaced by another kind of fear—a low, pervasive, sickening despair. How was I going to get out of here? What was I going to do now?

I sat up slowly. It hurt. Oh yeah, I remembered the pain too. The cuts and sores and bruises all over me, the ache all through me. Swallowing hard, I passed my hands over myself, checking the damage. I felt sore spots and frightening damp patches that might have been blood. But at least it didn't seem as if anything was broken.

My hand stopped at my belt when I felt the gun. Now I remembered that too.

I reached down and felt the space around me. Stone: slick, cold, and damp. I moved my hand and felt a small puddle of water. I scooped some up and splashed it into my mouth. It tasted metallic, but it eased my thirst.

I reached out until I felt a wall of stone. Slowly, holding on to the wall, I stood up. I felt wobbly. My legs felt weak. I leaned against the wall.

Now what? I was afraid to move. It was so utterly, so completely dark, there could've been an open pit in front of me and I never would've seen it. I could've taken one step and dropped into nothingness, a longer fall this time that would've really busted me to pieces. I could see myself lying broken and immobile in the blackness with no one to hear me screaming for help.

These and other images kept flashing in my mind as the scattered memories came back to me. The torture chair and the thugs with the acid syringe. My karate demonstration at school. Grabbing the rat-faced guy by the throat and running down the cinder block hallway, running for the black square that was the window. Talking to Beth in the cafeteria. Arguing with Alex in my mom's car. Stealing the truck to break out of the compound. The truck turning over. Grabbing the gun from the driver . . .

I caught my breath. There was something else I remembered now. Quickly, my hand went to my pants pocket. Yes, I felt it there. I reached inside and pulled it out: the keychain. The truck driver's keychain. I had taken it from the ignition to keep the bad guys from using the truck. Before I'd shoved it in my pocket, I had noticed it had a flashlight on it.

No matter how close I held the keychain to my face I couldn't see it, not even a little. I had to feel my way blindly along the shape of the keys, seeking out the flashlight. I moved my fingers carefully, resisting the urge to hurry. A frantic voice kept whispering in my head: *Don't drop it, don't drop it!* In this darkness, if I dropped the thing, there was no guarantee I would find it again.

But now, I felt it: the flashlight. My fingers made out its shape. I pressed the button. Hope sent my heart pounding wildly as a thin beam of white light shot blessedly through the dark. I shone it briefly around what turned out to be a small cave chamber. Then I pointed it up, looking for the place from which I'd fallen.

The hope in me died. I saw a slick, featureless slope of rock, too steep to climb without a rope. The narrow space through which I'd crawled was out of reach at the top of it. I could not get out the way I'd come in.

I scanned the light around the chamber again. There was only one other exit: a passage through the rock into more darkness. Everything inside me rebelled at the idea of going farther into the cave, moving away from the light and the air, dropping deeper into the earth.

But what choice did I have?

Much as I wanted to, I couldn't leave the flashlight on. I had to preserve the battery. For another moment or two, I let the light play over the entrance to the underground corridor, trying to memorize the path between the rocks that would get me there. Then, reluctantly, I released the button. The flashlight's beam vanished and the darkness was instantly complete again.

I began to edge forward, feeling my way along the wall of stone, trying to remember the path I'd seen in the light. Blind, utterly blind, I didn't dare to lift my feet, but shuffled slow-by-slow like an old, old man. Stubbing my toe on rocks, I felt my way around them. Now and then, I would shine the flashlight to see how far I'd come.

I reached the entrance to the corridor. I moved into it. Step by shuffling step, I made my way. Every few minutes, I would lift the flashlight again. Pierce the blackness with that narrow beam. I would memorize the next few steps and make sure there were no gaps or obstacles in my way. Then I would let the light die and shuffle forward, one hand clinging to the corridor wall.

I went on like that a long, long time. It seemed long, anyway. My clothes were damp and the cave was cold, and soon I was shivering, my teeth chattering. I had to force my mind away from the cold and from the pain all over my body—and from the hunger, too, sharp pangs of hunger that were now beginning to eat at my belly and make me weak.

Just concentrate on the movement, I told myself,

shivering. *Keep going. Never give in.* But as I edged deeper and deeper into that suffocating blackness, I heard another voice inside. Alex's voice. It came to me as if from the heart of the darkness, a furious, sizzling whisper: *It's all a lie. There's no hope. There's no sense trying. You're going to die down here, Charlie—down here in the dark where they'll never even find your corpse!*

Gritting my teeth, I forced Alex's voice into silence. I stopped again to scan the area with the flashlight. My hands were shaking so badly now I could hardly hold the keychain, even using both hands. My thumb rested on the button . . .

Then the flashlight slipped out of my grip!

It was an awful moment. So much had happened to me that day—the torture chair and the fear and the gunfire—but this was as bad as any of it. I heard the keychain hit the stone at my feet. Panicked, I crouched down after it. I moved my hand frantically over the stone floor. I couldn't find it. I could hear myself making a horrible whimpering noise. I didn't mean to, but it just came out of me.

"Please, please, please," I was saying.

Then there it was! I grabbed hold of the keychain as if it were a raft in the middle of the ocean. I stood up, trembling even worse than before, gripping that flashlight in my fist for dear life. For a long minute, I was afraid even to try again to find the button.

But I had to. I was completely disoriented now. I had no idea which direction to move in. Carefully—so carefully—I moved my thumb back to the flashlight button. I pressed it and shone the light in the dark.

I swallowed hard at what I saw. The corridor was narrowing down to nothing in front of me. No, not quite nothing. There was still a passage through the stone, but it was so tight I wasn't sure I could fit into it. And if I did fit into it, I wasn't sure I would be able to get out again.

But there was no hope behind me, so I had to go on. So I did.

I kept shuffling forward along the corridor, feeling the walls of it closing and closing on either side of me. Then I reached that narrow crevice. I put the flashlight into my pocket for safekeeping. I put my shoulder to the crevice opening. I squeezed my way in.

It was suffocating—almost unbearable. The rock walls pressed tight against my back and my face. I slid myself in farther, and with every inch I moved, the space got tighter. Soon I was gasping for breath as jutting rock pressed against my abdomen. It took an effort of both strength and willpower to keep cramming myself through the narrow space.

I couldn't reach the flashlight anymore. I couldn't even move my hands down to my pockets. I was pressed there like a butterfly in a book with no chance of breaking the stranglehold of the blackness. I couldn't see anything, not anything. I didn't know if the corridor would open again or simply end. And if it ended, I didn't know if I would be able to squeeze my way back out the way I came.

Still—still—I shoved my way deeper into that tomb of rock. And then, finally, it happened. I reached a passage so narrow, so tight, that even if I managed to force my way through it, I knew I could easily be wedged in there forever.

I stopped moving, held fast, the stone pressed tight against my face, my arms pinned in position with the hands up by my head. I could hardly move at all anymore. I could hardly breathe. And—I don't like saying this, but I have to tell the truth—I was now so terrified, so panicked, so frustrated and claustrophobic, that there were tears streaming down my face and I had to fight as hard as I could not to start blubbering like a child.

It was only a surge of anger that saved me. Anger and

desperation that flared up from my belly. I didn't want to die! Not here! Not like this!

So I bit down and an ugly noise squeezed out between my teeth as I shoved and worked my body even deeper into that black and narrow space. I was praying now, sort of a babbling, crazy prayer, snips and snatches of the Lord's Prayer and the Twenty-third Psalm and anything else I could remember, anything that shone a light of hope through my panic. I shoved and twisted and struggled and groaned and babbled, and the walls pressed so tight I thought *no, no, no,* I couldn't go another inch.

And then I broke through. Just like that. I squeezed past the narrow spot and the rock tomb seemed to open and release me. The breath came rushing back into my lungs. I stumbled once—and I was out of the corridor.

Relief made my legs go weak. I sank to one knee on the stone. Shivering uncontrollably, I tried to get my hand into my pocket, to get the flashlight, but I couldn't do it. I kept missing the pocket, my hand snaking out of control.

I put my hands under my arms to warm them. I knelt there like that, breathing hard, staring into the blackness.

And I saw something!

At first, I wasn't sure it was real. Even when I was sure, I could hardly believe it. I stared and blinked and stared again and there, for sure, it was. A patch of gray. A faint patch of gray in the near distance.

I swallowed hard. I tried to stay calm. I tried not to get my hopes up too much. I told myself: *Even if there's an opening, I might not be able to reach it. It might not be large enough for me to get through.*

But all the same, my heart was hammering as I climbed back to my feet. This time, I willed my hands steady. I went into my pocket and found the flashlight. I brought it out.

The thin beam of white light picked out an open chamber. There were rocks strewn here and there, but the passage across looked fairly easy. Even the chamber's ceiling was high, high enough so that I could walk without stooping. I jumped a little at a sudden fluttering noise. A bat had broken from its perch and flown to another. The beam picked out a whole cluster of the little creatures hanging up there in the dark.

I began to move again. Slow again. Preserving the flashlight battery. Picking out my path with the beam. Edging over the rock floor in the dark. I crossed the chamber. As I did, the patch of gray light on the far side grew nearer. As it grew nearer, it grew clearer and brighter, but still I couldn't see its source.

I kept moving toward it, inch by inch. My flashlight now picked out a jutting boulder. I put my hands on it and felt my way around it.

I don't think I have ever seen anything as beautiful as what I saw then. That circle of sunlight and blue sky. I thought it must've been something like what Lazarus saw when Death lost its hold on him. It felt like that to me, anyway. Like seeing a world of Life I thought I'd never see again.

It was another sinkhole in the cave ceiling, this one bigger than the one through which I'd come. A thin trickle of water was spilling over the edge of the gap. The droplets caught the light and twinkled as they fell. The sight of them was like visible music, like a song that you could see instead of hear. I laughed out loud at the sight. Or maybe I was weeping. I'm not really sure.

And the best thing—the best thing of all—was that the water was pouring down on what was almost a natural stairway formed by ledges and stones.

I moved toward that stairway wearily and began to climb up into the light.

CHAPTER SEVENTEEN

Angeline

"Angeline!"

A clear, sweet woman's voice came to me as if through a mist.

"Angeline! Where are you?"

I was lying with my face planted in a thin carpet of damp leaves. I had climbed out of the cave—I don't know—maybe fifteen minutes before. I was conscious, I guess, if you can call it that, but it was an awfully dim consciousness. Cold, exhausted, hungry—so hungry it was like a high, annoying siren going off in my brain. I couldn't seem to muster the energy to move anymore. I felt empty, as if I'd been hollowed out, as if there were no more muscle or bone or sinew inside me to give me the strength I needed.

"Angeline, sweetheart!"

I couldn't tell at first if that voice was real or something in my imagination. It was all mixed up with the other things swirling around in my brain: memories of the karate demonstration and the talk with Beth and the argument with Alex and then the rest: going home to dinner, writing my paper, IM'ing with Josh, and talking on the phone with Rick and then going to bed, my own bed, for the last time . . .

"Angeline! Where'd you go to, you mouse?"

For another few seconds, I lay half-awake and confused. I guess there was a part of me sort of hoping that voice was my mother's voice. Maybe she was calling my sister, Amy, and soon she'd call me to wake me up for another day at school.

"Wow," I'd tell her. "I had the weirdest dream . . ."

But then I took a deep breath and lifted my head out of the leaves and looked around me.

I was still in the forest, but it was different here. The trees were farther apart. They were mostly birch trees with peeling white bark. The underbrush was not as dense. There were open spaces covered with leaves. I could hear a brook bubbling happily nearby and birds chirping. The sun was low, but it wasn't blocked out of sight like it was before. I could see it clearly through the branches, a reddening ball among the clouds.

I turned my head to scan the area—and stopped.

There was a little girl standing there, gazing down at me.

She looked like she was about five years old. A solemn little creature with a pink woolen cap pulled down over her brown hair. She had a pink Windbreaker on and purple leggings marked with patches of dirt. She was holding a small ball in her hand. She was sort of turning the upper half of her body this way and that. She seemed mesmerized by the sight of me.

I stared at her as if she were a vision. I was half-afraid she was. Slowly, I pushed myself up onto my knees. I reached out to her. I wanted to touch her, to make sure she was real.

She just stood there, turning this way and that. She moved her gaze from my face and gazed at my reaching hand. She seemed fascinated by it, hypnotized.

I let my hand fall. I didn't want to frighten her. I

didn't want her to run away. I tried to smile. It wasn't easy. My face felt encrusted in dirt and pain.

"Hello," I managed to say. My voice sounded hoarse and rasping. "My name is Charlie. Charlie West. What's yours?"

The little girl hugged her ball tighter. She tucked her chin down as if she wanted to shrink up and hide behind the ball. She swiveled her body this way and that.

I kept staring at her. She was real, all right. She was really real. And if there was a little girl here, there must be an adult nearby, someone who could help me.

"Is someone with you?" I asked her, unable to keep my voice from trembling with hope. "Is your mother here . . . or someone?"

The little girl didn't answer. Only now did it occur to my muddled brain that the voice I'd heard, the woman calling, must be . . .

"Angeline! There you are!"

I followed the sound of her voice and saw her. A tall, slender lady in her thirties. A kind, pretty face with pretty red hair falling to her shoulders. She was wearing a navy-blue overcoat and jeans. Having finally found her daughter, she was stepping toward her. She hadn't seen me yet.

Then she did. She spotted me. She froze in her tracks. She stared at me with wide blue eyes.

She looked at her daughter again. Very quickly, she said, "Angeline! Angeline, come here right now. Come to Mommy right now!"

That broke the spell. Angeline turned away from me and ran to her mother, her pink sneakers crunching on the dead leaves. Clutching her ball in one hand, she clung to her mother's overcoat with the other and tried to hide in the folds of it.

The red-haired lady licked her lips. Staring at me, she began to back away. She was leaving me! She was going to leave me here!

"No! No, wait!" I said.

I managed to get to my feet, reaching out a hand to her. The mother took another step away, pulling her child with her.

I called out, more harshly than I meant to: "No! Stop! Don't go!"

The mother froze at the tone of my voice. She clutched her daughter to her more tightly. Her eyes traveled over me.

I took a stumbling step toward her.

"Please," she said. She spoke in a near-whisper, as

if she could barely get the words out. "Please don't hurt us."

I stopped moving. I'd been so desperate for help that it hadn't occurred to me what I must look like to her. A filthy, bloodstained, battered young man—and with a gun stuck in the waistband of his pants! I must've looked like some kind of madman or escaped convict or a killer or something. The sight of me must've terrified the poor woman out of her wits—but I hadn't thought of that.

"Hurt you?" I said, confused.

"Do you want money? I can give you some money. Please . . ."

"No, no . . ."

"Please. My daughter. She's just a child. You can do anything you want to me, but don't hurt her."

"Mommy!" the little girl cried out tearfully. She clutched her mother's coat tighter in fear.

Openmouthed, I stared at one of them and then the other. Finally, some understanding worked its way into my befuddled brain. My eyes misted over. I shook my head.

"No, no, no," I said. "Listen to me, listen. I swear to you, I swear: they could give me all the money in all the banks in all the world, and I wouldn't hurt a single hair on your head or on your daughter's. So help me. So help me."

She clutched her child even tighter. She took another step away, eyeing me suspiciously. "What do you want then?"

I stopped moving. I held up my hand to show I wouldn't come any closer. "Help. Please. I just need help."

The lady's lips trembled. Her eyes were swimming. She was so scared of me she was close to tears. I could see she was a nice lady, and it hurt my heart for her to be afraid of me. But I was desperate for her not to leave.

"What sort of help?" she asked. "I can give you some money. I don't have much. But I have some."

"Have you got a phone? If I could just call my mom and dad . . . They'll come and get me. They'll take me home. Please."

She licked her lips again. I saw her eyes go to the gun in my waistband. I put my hand on it.

The lady let out a cry of fear and turned her body to shield her daughter from a bullet.

"No, no, no—here!" I said. I drew the gun out of my waistband. I took it by the muzzle and held the handle out to her. "Here—take it."

There was another moment before she dared to turn

around and look. Then she did. A look of surprise came over her face as she saw me holding the gun out to her.

"Take it," I said. "I would never hurt you. Never. You've gotta believe me. I just want to go home. Please. Take the gun."

I could see in her eyes that she was confused now. She didn't know what to think of me. She just stood there, staring at the gun, trying to figure out what to do, how to protect her little girl.

Finally, she edged toward me cautiously. She reached for the gun gingerly, as if she was afraid I was trying to trap her, lure her in and grab her or something. When her fingers touched the gun, she snatched it quickly and leapt back out of my reach. She pointed the gun at me. It made me pretty nervous. It'd be just my luck today if I escaped from, like, a million guards and then got shot by a mom who pulled the trigger by mistake.

She just stood there, pointing the gun, not really knowing what to do next.

"Look," I said. "There are men after me. Bad men— dangerous. I don't know how far away they are, but they may still be looking for me. If I could just use your phone . . ."

Holding the gun on me, the lady swallowed. "It's . . .

It's in the car," she said uncertainly. "I don't have it with me." Then she added: "It doesn't work out here anyway. There's no signal."

"Well, listen, I really need to call . . ."

"All right, all right," she said. She thought some more. I could see she was making a plan. "You can come with me. We can drive back down the road. It usually picks up a signal at the bottom."

I nodded. "Great. That'd be great, ma'am, really. Uh . . . Do you think you could stop pointing the gun at me now?"

She looked down at her hand as if she'd forgotten the gun was there. When she saw it, she considered it a long moment. Finally, I guess she came to a decision. She took a deep breath. She slipped the gun into the pocket of her overcoat. I took a deep breath too, relieved.

"Okay," she said. "Come with me."

CHAPTER EIGHTEEN

Dateline

I followed her out of the woods. It wasn't easy. I was hurting all over and walking slowly. A few times, the red-haired lady had to wait up for me, even though she was walking with the little girl. She'd pause and watch me hobbling as fast as I could, trying to catch up with her, and I thought I saw a little mom-like sympathy come into her eyes. It was a nice thing to see. I was in need of a little mom-like sympathy at that point.

When we came out of the trees, there was a rolling slope of dirt and grass. There were picnic benches here and a rusted, dilapidated swing set. After everything that had happened, it was the oddest sight to see. So normal, you know. If it hadn't been for the pain and the blood and the muck all over me, I would've wondered if my whole ordeal that day had been a dream.

Beyond the grass there was a dirt parking place. There was only the one car there—her car, a Ford Explorer, just like my mom's, even colored brown like my mom's.

I waited while the red-haired lady strapped the little girl into the child seat in back.

"Is the man bad, Mommy?" I heard the little girl ask softly.

"No," the red-haired lady said. "He just needs help. Don't worry. Everything's going to be fine."

I sat in the front passenger seat as the lady drove over a narrow dirt road. It was a long road, strewn with rocks, and slow going. The Explorer bounced and jarred as it hit holes in the earth and up-sticking boulders. Every bounce went through my body in a flash of pain.

The lady and I were silent at first. But then I decided to try to make conversation. I wanted her to see I was a good guy so she wouldn't be so scared of me.

"My mom has an Explorer too," I said to her. "It's the same color."

She glanced over at me. I thought maybe she started to smile for a second, but I guess she stopped herself.

"I'm really sorry I scared you," I said. "I guess I must look pretty gnarly at this point."

She glanced over again. Things were improving, I could tell. She was a mom, you know, like my mom, so I could kind of read her, tell what she was thinking. She had that little quirk at the corner of her lips that moms get when they don't want to forgive you for something but they can't help it.

"My name's Charlie," I told her. "Charlie West. I go to Spring Hill North."

She peered out through the windshield, the Explorer bouncing and tossing over the boulder-strewn path. "I'm Cathy Simmons," she said finally.

"I really appreciate you helping me, Mrs. Simmons. I don't know what I would've done if you hadn't come along. Thanks."

This time, she took a longer look at me, more curious, you know. I think she was beginning to get it. I think she was beginning to see I was just a kid, maybe like some of the kids she knew.

"What on earth happened to you, Charlie?" she asked. "When I saw you in the woods . . ."

"I know, I know. I must look like a zombie or something."

"Or something—yeah. What happened? What are you doing with a gun?"

I shook my head. "I know this is gonna sound weird, but . . . I don't know what happened, Mrs. Simmons. I've been trying to figure it out. I mean, some guys must've captured me in my sleep or something. I went to bed last night at home and I just woke up today and . . . everything was crazy. They had me tied up and were trying to kill me and I had to run for it and there was this cave . . ." I couldn't explain it, couldn't put the words together. Just thinking about it made me all confused and upset. I ran my hand up through my hair. I could feel the dirt and twigs tangled in it. "It was pretty bad," I said.

She gave me another "mom look": it was the one they give you when they don't believe you, when they can see you're making up a story to get out of trouble and they don't want to call you a liar but they don't want you to think you've fooled them either.

"It's true!" I said—which is pretty much what you say to moms when they give you that look. It sort of comes out automatically. But then I had to admit: "I guess it does sound pretty lame."

Mrs. Simmons nodded, but one corner of her mouth lifted in a kind of wry mom smile. "Where are you from, Charlie? Where are your mom and dad?"

"I guess they're back home. In Spring Hill."

She shook her head. "I don't know it."

"It's the Whitney County seat."

She gave me a strange look. Then she said: "You're a long way from home. We're just north of Centerville here."

I gaped at her. "Centerville? No way! That's on the other side of the state!"

That got me another soothing blast of "mom sympathy." Then Mrs. Simmons nodded her head at the glove compartment. "The phone's in there. Why don't you see if you can get a signal?"

I got out her cell, a Razr. I flipped it open.

"No," I said. "No service."

"All right," said Mrs. Simmons. "It's always bad up in here. Wait till we get to the bottom of this road."

I nodded. I leaned back against the seat. I was too tired to talk anymore. In fact, I'd never felt so tired in my life. I was hungry, too, really hungry now. I wondered if I could talk Mrs. Simmons into giving me some food or if I'd have to wait for my mom and dad to come get me.

In the seat behind me, the little girl, Angeline, began to sing. She had a doll back there she was playing with, and she was sort of singing to it and herself in a low voice. I guess it gets pretty boring strapped into those child seats.

I leaned my head back and listened to her rambling little song. I started to drift off into sleep, but then I felt myself strapped to the torture chair and saw the rat-faced guy coming at me with his syringe . . .

"Charlie!"

I felt a hand on my shoulder. I sat up suddenly. A strap pulled tight against my chest, holding me in place. For a second, I thought I really *was* back in the torture chair, that my whole escape had been a dream . . .

But no. I looked around. I was still in the Explorer. Mrs. Simmons was sitting next to me. She smiled gently.

"You fell asleep."

"Yeah," I said. "Yeah. I guess I did."

"We're here."

I looked around, dazed. The car had stopped. We were in the driveway of a small house, a brown clap-board house on a wooded road. I could see a couple of other houses, but they were far away, all but hidden in the trees.

"This is where I live," she said. Her voice sounded different now. It was nicer somehow, warmer. I guess she'd had time to think about it while I was asleep and had decided I was okay. "You can come in and use the phone inside," she told me.

It felt strange to be inside her house—in a normal house where nice, regular people lived—it felt good. There were pictures on the wall and photographs of her and her husband over the fireplace. There was even a big old yellow Labrador who met us at the door, sniffed me up and down, and gave a throaty little cough of approval before slobbering all over Angeline and making her laugh.

The kitchen was especially nice, all homey and old-fashioned with yellow-and-white floor tiles and red-and-white curtains and a view of the forest through the window over the sink. It made me feel almost like I was at one of my friends' houses or something.

Mrs. Simmons gestured to a phone that was standing in a charger on the kitchen counter. I went to it. Mrs. Simmons, meanwhile, told Angeline to sit down at the kitchen table. Angeline sat there and talked to her doll, and Mrs. Simmons went to the refrigerator to get her a snack.

"Do you want anything to eat, Charlie?" she asked over her shoulder.

I had to swallow a whole mouthful of drool before I could croak, "Yeah. Please."

She stopped with her hand on the refrigerator and gave me the sympathy look again. Then, kind of quietly, she nodded at the phone and said, "Don't forget to use the area code."

I nodded. I dialed home. While I waited for the phone to ring, my heart started beating harder. I was crazy excited. Just to hear my mom's voice or my dad's . . . Just to know they were coming to get me . . . I almost didn't care anymore how I'd gotten here or what had happened. Just as long as it was over. Just as long as I could go home.

The phone started ringing. Then my breath caught as the ringing stopped and a woman's voice came over the line.

"Mom?" I said.

But the voice said only: "We're sorry. This number has been disconnected. Please check the number and dial again." It was a recording.

Confused, I looked over at Mrs. Simmons. She was setting a juice box and a Pop-Tart in front of Angeline.

"That's weird," I said.

She moved to the refrigerator again. "What's weird?"

I didn't answer. I redialed my home number, making

sure I got it right. This time, the phone didn't even ring. There was just the voice: "We're sorry. This number has been disconnected . . ."

I lowered the phone from my ear.

"What? What's the matter?" asked Mrs. Simmons.

"They say the number's been disconnected."

Mrs. Simmons shrugged. "Might be some problem on the line. What about their cell phones?"

"I don't know the numbers. They were on my speed dial—I never had to memorize them."

"Well, why don't you just call the sheriff's department? They'll contact your folks for you. You're going to need to talk to them anyway if there are all these bad guys you say are after you."

"There are!" I insisted.

"Well, okay," said Mrs. Simmons—she still sounded doubtful. "Then call the sheriff."

"Yeah," I said. "Yeah, that's a good idea."

I looked down at the phone in my hand. I hesitated. I could just imagine trying to explain to a bunch of policemen what had happened to me. *Well, I went to bed and when I woke up* . . . Right. I could just imagine how crazy I'd sound and the way they'd look at me, like I was some lying kid.

"Here," Mrs. Simmons said, coming to me. "I'll call them. My husband's an assistant district attorney. They all know me."

"Oh, great," I said, relieved. I handed her the phone. At least she could tell them I wasn't a bad guy.

"You sit down and eat something," she told me. "I put some chicken out for you. You must be starved."

She gestured at the table. I saw now she'd poured a glass of milk for me and put a couple of pieces of chicken and a Pop-Tart on a plate. The sight of the food just about blew everything else out of my mind. My mouth hung open as I sat down at the table. I stared at the food as if it were some kind of vision: a drumstick, a breast, a Pop-Tart with strawberry frosting. I said a quick grace in my head—very quick. My mouth was watering so much, I had to wipe it before I could start to eat.

"Jack! Hi, it's Cathy Simmons," Mrs. Simmons said into the phone. She went on talking as she carried the phone out into the living room. I couldn't hear what she said.

Didn't matter. I wasn't paying attention anymore anyway. I was lifting that drumstick. I was biting into it. For a second, the taste of the food was so powerful it made my head swim. I hesitated, afraid I was going to throw up. But then my stomach settled and I started eating for real. By which I mean: I ripped into that drumstick like Godzilla devouring a tourist. The drumstick, then the breast, then the Pop-Tart . . .

"You're sloppy," said Angeline, watching me from across the table as I gobbled the food.

I winked at her. "Hungry," was all I could manage to say as I ate. Then I hit the glass of milk. It went bubbling down my throat in a single gulp.

A second later, Mrs. Simmons came back into the room. By then my plate was just about spotless. I was busy pressing my finger to it to get up whatever last Pop-Tart crumbs I could find.

Mrs. Simmons carried the phone to the charger and set it there. Her back was to me and she stayed like that another second or two. Then she turned around and smiled at me—only it wasn't the same sort of smile as before. She looked different now. I noticed it right away. Some of the color was gone from her cheeks and the softness from her eyes. She looked pale and worried. Her smile was a forced smile.

"Well . . . um, Charlie," she said. "Would you like to clean up a little? Maybe even take a shower. You're about my husband's size. I could put out some fresh clothes for you."

I thought about it. A shower would feel awfully nice. Plus I wouldn't smell so bad when my folks came for me. "Sure," I said. "Is everything all right? Did you reach the sheriff?"

"What? Oh. Oh, yes. Yes, everything's fine." I could see Mrs. Simmons's eyes go back and forth as if she were searching for the right thing to say. "The deputies are on their way. It's a bit of a drive from town, but they'll be here soon."

"Great," I said. "You think I should wait to take a shower in case they . . ."

"No," Mrs. Simmons said quickly. Then she did a strange thing. She went to the table and scooped Angeline up into her arms. She held her protectively, as if she were afraid of me again, afraid I might hurt them. "No, you just go on into the back room and take a shower like I say. I'll lay some clothes out on the sofa for you, all right?"

I was kind of confused by her behavior, but I said, "Sure."

The back room was on the ground floor at the other end of the house. It was a bright room with flowered wallpaper and a sofa. There was a small wooden table with a sewing machine on it. And there was an easy chair with a newspaper lying on it. I could see the headline: "Homeland Secretary to Meet with President on Terror."

Still clutching Angeline in her arms, Mrs. Simmons pointed me to the bathroom on the room's far wall.

"Right in there," she said. "Go ahead, there are towels and everything, and I'll bring you some clothes."

Then she went out—hurried out, I thought—closing the door behind her.

I thought she was acting strange, but then the whole situation was so strange, I shrugged it off again. I went into the bathroom. It was pleasant and homey like the rest of the house. Big fluffy towels hanging on racks. A flowered shower curtain. White tiles on the walls with blue designs on them.

I got the shower going and started to unbutton my shirt. It would be good to get out of my clothes, wet and dirty and bloody as they were. As I worked the buttons, I turned without thinking to look in the mirror over the bathroom sink.

I stopped moving. I stood stock-still. My hand froze on one of the buttons.

My face. The face staring back at me from the mirror. It was me—I mean, I recognized myself, but . . . but I'd changed. A lot. My face was leaner, sharper, stronger-looking. And my beard . . . I looked like I hadn't shaved for a day or two, but instead of the patches of fuzz I usually got, my beard was coming in all over, heavy and full.

I stood there staring at my reflection and this thought—this impossible thought—came into my head.

I was older. I looked older, anyway. I looked older than I did when I went to bed at home last night.

The shower went on running as I stood there. Steam began to seep out from behind the shower curtain. Slowly the mirror began to fog over, the white mist moving in from the edges toward the center. I watched as the reflection of my face was covered until only the eyes were staring out at me. Then the eyes were gone too. I was just a shadow in the mist.

That broke the spell. I turned away from the mirror quickly. I hurried out of the bathroom, out into the other room with the sofa and the sewing table.

There was the easy chair. There was the newspaper on it. I went to the chair. I picked up the paper.

"HOMELAND SECRETARY TO MEET WITH PRESIDENT ON TERROR."

Above the headline was the date. I could still remember the date from yesterday. A Wednesday in September.

An ordinary Wednesday. It ought to be Thursday now.

And it was. It was Thursday. Only it was October. I thought, *Wow, a whole month has passed!*

Then my eyes traveled just a little farther, and I saw the rest.

It was October, but a year later. A year had passed since I went to bed last night.

It was one full year since the last day I remembered.

CHAPTER NINETEEN
Police

I stood in the shower. The hot water streamed down over me. It felt good, really good. The heat seeped into my aching muscles, soothing them. It stung on my cuts and bruises, but it was a good sting, a cleansing sting. The stream drove the dirt and blood off me. I stood with my head down, watching as the dark, gritty water swirled down the drain.

I stared and I thought: *A year!* How was it possible? A year of my life had vanished. My eighteenth birthday had come and gone and I couldn't even remember it.

I tried. I tried to remember. Something. Anything. I strained as hard as I could to bring any of it back. But there was nothing there. As far as my mind was concerned, I had gone to bed last night and woken up strapped to a chair. If a year had passed in the meantime, it was lost to me completely. I had no memory of it at all.

I put my hands over my face. I rubbed my eyes. I tried again to make some sense out of the events of the day, sifting through them for any clue I could find. I thought back to that first moment, the moment I had woken up in the chair. What had happened before that? Wasn't there something? Anything?

I couldn't come up with it. I turned off the shower. I stepped out and grabbed one of the towels and began to dry myself off. And now there was . . . just a trace . . . a hint, a whisper of a memory coming back to me.

It had happened when I first woke up. When I first found myself strapped to that chair. Everything was confusion and fear and pain inside me. But there were voices. I remembered now. There were voices talking just outside the cell door. What did they say? I tried to remember. Maybe there was a clue there—a clue to where a year of my life had gone.

I stepped out of the bathroom. Just as Mrs. Simmons

had promised, she'd put some clothes on the sofa for me, a pair of jeans and a flannel work shirt. There were also some clean socks and a pair of old sneakers. There was even some underwear in a package that hadn't been opened yet.

I started to get dressed. All the while, I was thinking, trying to remember, trying to call back those voices I'd heard.

Homelander!

Yes. That was something. It came back to me now. Someone had said the word *Homelander. Homelander One*—as if there were more of them, a lot of Homelanders. What did it mean? I had no idea.

What else? My name. Yes. Someone had said my name.

West.

I closed my eyes as I dressed, trying to bring back the scene, trying to bring back the words.

Orton knows the bridge as well as West.

My head was beginning to throb. That was all I could come up with for now. I finished dressing. I sat on the sofa and put the old sneakers on. Everything fit pretty well. I was grateful to be clean and grateful for the feel of fresh clothing.

I opened the door to the back room and stepped out into the hallway.

"Mrs. Simmons?" I called.

There was no answer. It was odd. The house had an empty feel to it suddenly. I waited a second. Then I started down the hall, calling as I went.

"Mrs. Simmons? I'm done with my shower. Are the deputies here yet?"

I came out into the living room. It was a big room, two stories tall with a cathedral ceiling. There was a fireplace against one wall. Chairs: a rocking chair, a couple of armchairs. Another sofa. A wide-screen TV.

But it was empty here too. There was no one around.

I was about to call out again—about to head into the kitchen—when I noticed something. There was this large picture window on one wall. It looked out at the front of the house, out at the quiet street and the forest across the way and the first dark of evening coming into the sky above the trees. The carport was around the side of the house out of sight, but you could see part of the driveway leading up to it. There were cars there now. Cars that hadn't been there before. I moved closer to the window and looked out. There was a blue Cadillac and a red-and-white sheriff's department cruiser and another car in front of those that I couldn't make out, and two more cruisers parked at the curb down the street.

Good, they're here, I thought. But where? Where was Mrs. Simmons? Where were all the deputies from those cars? Where was everyone?

I turned around, starting to call, "Mrs. Simmons . . . !"

And suddenly I was looking down the barrel of a large handgun, pressed close to my forehead.

"Freeze, West!" a man shouted in my face. "You move and I'll blow your head off!"

I froze. I gaped into the black bore of the gun barrel.

"Put your hands up! Put 'em up! Now! Now!"

I swallowed. I raised my hands. I was scared—of course: someone points a gun at you and you get scared, that's just the way it is. But I wasn't as scared as you might think. I was really just startled mostly. I could see now that the man holding the gun was wearing a brown khaki uniform. He was a sheriff's deputy, a lawman, one of the good guys. I realized there must be some mistake.

"It's okay," I said, holding my hands in the air. "It's just me. I gave the gun to Mrs. . . ."

"Shut up! Put your hands behind your head!"

This was another voice. I turned to it. Another

deputy was standing by the kitchen door. He had a gun, too, and it was also leveled at me.

"Do it! Do it now!"

Yet a third voice. A third deputy was coming out of the hall—where I'd just come from. Another gun was aimed my way.

"Okay, okay," I said. "Don't shoot. I'm the good guys." I put my hands behind my head.

And with breathtaking speed, the three deputies leapt at me.

"Hey!" I shouted.

They spun me around. One of them hit me in the back of the legs so that I dropped to my knees. Another one wrestled my hands down from my head and twisted them painfully behind my back. I felt a cold pinch of metal as he snapped handcuffs on my wrists.

"Ow! What're you doing?" I said.

"Shut up! On your feet, West!"

Even as he was shouting in my ear, he was dragging me up off my knees, onto my feet. It was hard to maneuver with my hands cuffed behind me.

One of the deputies was murmuring into the microphone clipped to his shoulder.

"All clear. We got him!"

Through the window, I could see more deputies coming into view, coming out from where they'd been hiding behind trees and against the wall of the house. They were all wearing bulletproof vests. A couple of them were carrying assault rifles. Who'd they think I was? Osama bin Laden?

Everything was happening fast—so fast I couldn't think, couldn't figure out what was going on. The deputies were shoving me toward the door, shouting at me.

"Move! Come on! Move it! Go!"

They shoved me to the front door of the house. One of the deputies outside opened it. The others half shoved and half carried me through, outside into the evening.

There were deputies on every side of me. My eyes went from one to another, looking for someone who would explain, some friendly face.

"What're you doing?" I said. "What's the matter?"

"Shut up," someone answered.

Then I heard someone growl angrily, "You lousy punk . . ."

And suddenly a man was in front of me. Not a deputy. A broad-shouldered man about my height wearing a suit and tie. He had a square head like a cement block. He had little eyes and they were black with anger. He grabbed the front of my shirt, taking a handful of flesh with it.

"If I find out you laid one hand on my wife or my kid, you little punk, not even the cops'll be able to protect you." He was so close, I could feel his spit on my face as he talked. "I'll find you wherever you are, I'll . . . !"

"Harmon!" I heard a woman shout. She sounded as if she was crying. I tried to turn to her. It was hard with this guy grabbing me. But I caught a glimpse of some red hair off to my right. It was Mrs. Simmons.

The guy grabbing me shouted again. "You hear what I'm telling you, punk?"

"I didn't—" I started to say.

But before I could finish, a deputy took hold of the guy and pulled him off me. He had to work at it. The guy didn't want to let go. The deputy had to wrap one arm around his neck and use the other hand to pry the guy's fingers out of the fabric of my shirt. Finally, the guy released me and the deputy dragged him away.

I stumbled backward, but another deputy held me up.

And now, before I could think, yet another man was approaching me. This was a great big guy. He seemed almost to be bursting out of his khaki uniform. He towered over me. He had a huge belly that came on before him like a prow goes before a ship.

It was the sheriff himself. His badge said so. He was older—I figured about sixty or so—with sparse gray hair swept back over the dome of his egg-shaped head. He had a large, wrinkled face that looked like it smiled a lot. But it wasn't smiling now.

"Easy does it, Harmon," he said calmly. He was looking down at me, but he was talking to the other guy, the guy who'd grabbed me. "Your girls are fine. The boy didn't hurt them any."

"I didn't!" I said.

Wild-eyed, I looked to my right. The guy—Harmon—was standing there next to Mrs. Simmons. He had his arm wrapped protectively around her. She in turn had her arm around the little girl, Angeline, and was leaning her face against Harmon's jacket and crying. I guessed Harmon was her husband, the assistant district attorney. He was glaring at me with those small, furious black eyes. Sneering at me with his lips working as if he still had a lot he wanted to say.

I looked up at the sheriff. "What's going on?" I said. "I didn't do anything. What's going on?"

The sheriff had a calm, quiet voice. He sounded like

a man who didn't get upset much. "I think you know what's going on, son, don't you?"

I shook my head. "I don't, I swear."

"You are Charlie West, right?" he asked me.

I nodded.

"Charlie West from Spring Hill."

"That's right."

He sort of cocked his head to one side as if to say: *That settles it then.*

"Well, Charlie," he said slowly. "I'm Sheriff James. And you're done, that's all. You're going back to prison where you belong."

"Prison?" I said. My voice cracked as I said it. A million thoughts were racing through my mind. Was that where I'd escaped from? Had I been in prison when I woke up this morning? No! They don't strap you down to chairs and torture you in prison—not in an American prison, anyway. These people around me weren't the same people who had chased me through the forest earlier. These were deputies. This was the law, the good guys. They were supposed to be on my side. "Why should I go to prison?" I asked him.

Sheriff James gave a little laugh. "That's where we generally send folks who've been convicted of murder."

My mouth opened and closed silently. I could only barely force out a whisper: "Murder. What do you mean?"

"I mean you're a killer," said the big man with a heavy nod. "You were tried in a court of law and convicted by a jury of the murder of Alex Hauser."

PART TWO

CHAPTER TWENTY

Rose

Morning came, and the cell door opened. I was sitting on the edge of the cot with my head in my hands. I looked up and a deputy was standing over me, a giant of a man with a face like granite.

"Come on, West," he said. "Let's go."

I stood up wearily, slowly, aching and stiff in every muscle. My wounds had been treated when I was brought into jail, but I still hurt all over. I stepped out of the cell. The deputy put my hands behind my back and handcuffed me again. Then he took hold of my elbow and led me down the hallway.

It had been a long, long night. The police had taken my clothes away and made me dress in an orange jumpsuit with COUNTY JAIL stamped on the back of it. I'd tried and tried to tell them I was innocent. I'd made my voice hoarse trying to tell them. But no one would listen. They'd dragged me to the cell and threw me in and walked away.

The cell was hardly bigger than a closet. There was just a narrow cot bolted to the wall, a steel toilet in one corner and a steel sink. Instead of bars, the door was a big piece of Plexiglas with airholes in it. There was a security camera hanging up in the hall outside, looking right in at me. It took pictures of me every second. Even when I went to the bathroom, the camera watched me. It was humiliating. It made me feel as if I weren't a human being, as if I were a rat in a cage being observed for a laboratory experiment or something.

I hardly slept at all. Whenever I did sleep, nightmares swarmed through my brain. In the nightmares, there were faces, grinning, leaning in on me. There were voices whispering:

. . . *Homelander One.*

We'll never get another shot at Yarrow.

. . . two more days . . .

. . . can send Orton . . .

. . . knows the bridge as well as West.

But when I woke up the voices were gone. They trailed away like wisps of smoke, and I could barely remember them or what they'd said. Whatever was left of the nightmares was crowded out of my mind by the nightmare reality around me: this cell, this cot, this jail.

You were tried in a court of law and convicted by a jury of the murder of Alex Hauser.

I still couldn't comprehend it, couldn't take it in. A year of my life had vanished. Alex was dead. They thought I had killed him. I'd been *convicted* of killing him. It wasn't just the bad guys—the Homelanders—who were after me. It was the good guys too. The police. Everyone.

By the time morning broke, I was exhausted. As the deputy led me down the hall, I was too tired to ask questions, too tired to do anything but go wherever he took me. We went down the hall in silence. Neither of us said a word.

He brought me into a large, messy room. There were several gunmetal-gray desks arrayed around. A lot of papers tacked to the wall. There were men sitting at the desks, men in suits and ties. They stopped talking as I entered, wearing my orange jumpsuit. They watched curiously as the deputy led me past them. He took me to a far corner of the room and through another door.

We came into a smaller room, almost as small as my cell. There was nothing in here but a heavy wooden table and three plastic chairs. There was grimy white soundproofing on the walls. A fluorescent light hung from the ceiling. Now and then, it snapped and flickered. In a corner of the ceiling there was a security camera, just like the one outside my cell. A red light burned on top of it as it took its pictures.

The deputy helped me sit down in the chair behind the heavy table. He uncuffed my hands so I could bring them out from behind my back, but then he handcuffed my right hand to a rail set into one side of the table. That way, I couldn't break free and run for it.

Then the deputy walked out of the room and left me there.

I sat in silence, handcuffed to the table. I felt empty and hollow and alone. Ten minutes went by. It felt like an hour. Then the door opened, and a man came in.

He was a black guy. Not big, shorter than me, but he was trim, and you could see he was in good shape. He was wearing a sort of colorless suit with a bright blue shirt and a tie that looked like the TV picture when the satellite goes on the fritz. He had a round face with a high forehead and short hair, flat features and a thin mustache. He had very steady eyes. You could see he was smart just looking in his eyes. He was smart and cool and nothing fooled him.

He had a big black binder in one hand. It was filled with papers. I could see some numbers on the back of it and my name: West, Charlie.

He dropped the black binder on the table in front of me. It made a loud *whap* when it fell.

"Well, well, well," he said. His voice was like his eyes, smart and cool and not very friendly. "Charlie West. We meet again at last."

I narrowed my eyes at him. I'd never seen him before.

"I'm sorry," I said. My voice came out so soft and hoarse, I had to clear my throat and start again: "I'm sorry. I don't know you. I don't know who you are."

The man gave a short laugh. He looked around as if someone else were standing there, as if he wanted to share the joke.

"You don't know me, huh," he said.

"I . . . I don't remember."

"Oh, come on. It hasn't been that long, Charlie." He waited a few seconds as if it would all come back to me. I didn't say anything. What could I say? A moment passed and the fluorescent above us snapped and flickered. There was a little dance of shadows then a pale, sickly light. After a while, the man took a deep breath as if he was fighting down his anger. "Well, let me introduce myself," he said. "I'm Detective Rose." He waited again as if that would refresh my memory. It didn't. "I'm the man who arrested you for the Hauser killing."

I shook my head wearily. I rubbed my eyes with my free hand. It hardly seemed worth saying again, but I had to say it. "I didn't kill Alex!" I thumped my fist on the table as the words came out.

Detective Rose gave a little smile, a cold smile with no feeling in it. He pulled out one of the other chairs. Propped his foot up on it. He looked down at me. "Yes, you did, Charlie. Witnesses said you did. Murder weapon with your prints and DNA said you did. Blood on your clothes said you did. Jury said you did." He made a little gesture with his hand. "So you did."

It was all so insane, so horribly, frustratingly insane, that I actually laughed. It was a miserable laugh, but a laugh all the same. "I don't remember any of that," I said.

"I don't remember you. I don't remember a jury. I didn't even know Alex was dead till the sheriff told me. The last time I saw him, we were talking. In my car by the park. Then I went home. I went to bed and I woke up in this room . . ."

"Strapped to a chair, yeah. You told the deputies last night."

"I don't remember anything else. I don't remember a whole year. A whole year of my life is gone!"

"Well, that's very convenient, isn't it?" He took his foot off the chair, turned the chair around and straddled it. That brought him down to my level so I was looking straight into those smart, cool eyes. "You murder your friend. You break out of prison. You outrun me for more than three months, and it's all . . ." He waved his hand dreamily. "Gone. Like a dream."

"It is. There's nothing there." I stared at him, shaking my head. "But it doesn't matter. It doesn't make sense. I would never murder anyone. And Alex . . . he was my friend. I keep telling you."

The fluorescent light crackled and flickered. The cold smile played at the detective's lips again. "Yeah, you keep telling me," he said. "You told me when we first brought you in. He was your friend. Except he threatened you, didn't he? You were going out with his girl and he didn't like it, and him and a couple of his boys threatened to bounce you around for it."

"Oh yeah, but that was . . ."

"And then you took a drive together and you fought with him."

"We didn't fight, exactly, we . . ."

"Witnesses saw it, Charlie. They heard you yelling."

I looked away from that cool stare. I remembered that much. I remembered Alex and I yelling at each other and the lady with the dog turning at the sound of our loud, angry voices.

"Then you followed him into the park," said Detective Rose. "And you stabbed him to death."

"No!" I shook my right fist so that my handcuff rattled against the rail. The words came tearing out of my mouth in a shout. "I didn't."

"How do you know? I thought you couldn't remember anything."

"I remember that!"

"Oh, that's convenient. You just forgot everything else, everything but your innocence."

"I didn't do it. I wouldn't do it. I'm not a killer!"

The fluorescent light went out for half a second, and

when it came back on the detective's face had changed. The cool smile was gone and an angry sneer had taken its place beneath the thin mustache.

"You want to know something funny, Charlie?" he said. "I been a cop a long time. Worked the big city before I came to Spring Hill. I've arrested a lot of people, a lot of bad people, some really bad. But I never had any feelings about them one way or the other. They did what they did, I did what I did, we all knew the rules of the game. But you, Charlie . . ." He stood up, pushing the chair away from him so it scraped against the floor. "With you it was different." He sneered down at me. His mouth worked as if he wanted to spit out a bad taste. "I don't like you, Charlie. And I'll tell you why. It's not 'cause you lied to me. All you murdering punks lie, that's nothing. But you lied to me and I believed you. That's what it is. You looked me in the eye with that all-American face of yours, and I believed you were just who you said you were, just who everybody said you were. The decent kid. The kid who gets it. The kid who works hard and does right. The kid who walks like a man—like a man oughta walk, anyway. I believed you were that kid, Charlie. You fooled me. And I don't know, but somehow I can't forgive you for that. And I'll never let it happen again."

"Look at me," I said to him. I pleaded with him. I lifted my hands so the handcuff on my right wrist pulled tight. "Please, Detective Rose, look at me. I'm scarred, bruised, beaten up. There are burns on me . . . look!" I tried to twist my handcuffed arm to show him. "Right there. Burns. Something happened to me. You can see that! I was captured. There were people . . . in the woods. A whole compound. They called themselves Homelanders. They hurt me. They tried to kill me. Why would I make it up?"

He laughed, but there was no humor in it. "You've been making things up since the first time I talked to you. Everything you say is made up. Far as I can tell, your whole life is a lie."

"If you could just . . . call my parents. Really—they'll tell you . . ."

With a loud snap, the fluorescent light flashed off and on. In that split second of darkness, Detective Rose leapt forward so that the next time I saw him, he was right up against the table, looming over me. At the same moment, he slapped his hand angrily down on the table.

"Your parents aren't gonna help you," he said through his teeth. "You were tried as an adult, convicted as an adult. You got twenty-five years to life for murder, and they're sure to tack on more 'cause you ran away."

"I didn't do anything!" I cried up at him. "I don't remember anything! I don't know what's happening! Please! Please!"

Despair flooded up through me. The fluorescent light flickered and snapped. The handcuffs rattled as I leaned my elbows on the table and buried my face in my hands.

"Please," I said again. "Somebody's gotta believe me."

But when I looked up, Detective Rose had moved away from me to the door. He was still sneering. Shaking his head as if he was disgusted by what a low creature I was.

"It's going to be a pleasure to take you back to prison, Charlie," he said. "And I plan to make personally certain that you don't get out again until you're an old, old man."

CHAPTER TWENTY-ONE

A Voice in the Crowd

The granite-faced deputy came and took me back to my cell. He brought me a breakfast of hash and coffee. I was hungry enough to eat it. It lay on my stomach like lead.

When I was done, I sat on the edge of the cot. I stared down at the cell's stone floor.

It's a funny thing when despair gets to you. It doesn't even feel like despair. You don't think to yourself: *Oh, I have no hope. Oh, I give up. Oh, there's nothing I can do.* That's just everyday complaining. That's just feeling sorry for yourself.

Real despair is different. It creeps up on you in disguise. It comes as a kind of sleepiness, a kind of heavy sadness that weighs you down. It makes you lazy. It makes you just want to go along, drift with the current of events, drift and drift as if you were lying on a raft floating down a river on a sweet summer day. Whatever happens, you don't fight it. You just go where events take you and then sit and wait for the next event to take you on.

That's what I did. I sat and waited. I didn't say to myself: *Don't give up.* I didn't say: *Remember the Churchill Card. Never give in.* I didn't really say much of anything to myself anymore. I was just too tired. I was just waiting for the next thing. They were coming to take me to prison. I was going to be behind bars for the next twenty-five years, maybe more. What was the use in fighting it? No one would believe me. No one would help me. Nothing to do but just drift along.

After a while, I lay back on the cot and dozed.

I don't know if I had another nightmare. Maybe I did. All I'm sure of is that suddenly my eyes were wide open and my heart was hammering in my chest and there was a clammy sweat on my face. I swallowed hard, staring up at the stone ceiling. A weird and terrible thought began to work its way into my mind.

Everything you say is made up. Your whole life is a lie.

The thought was kind of like a whisper, as if someone invisible were crouching next to me with his lips to my ear, whispering very low. The whisper was so low I didn't really even hear the words at first. Slowly, they just sort of worked their way into my consciousness until I was aware of them.

Your whole life is a lie. That's what Detective Rose had said to me.

And now the whisper was saying to me, *What if he's right? What if it's true?*

It was a good question, wasn't it? What if Detective Rose was right? What if everything I thought was true was a lie and everything I thought was a lie was really true? I mean, what if I did kill Alex? What if I was a phony, just pretending to be a good guy when really I was the worst, the lowest, a killer? What if everything I believed about myself, everything I remembered about my life, was false? It was possible, wasn't it? I mean, I couldn't remember a whole year. How could I tell whether the things I *did* remember had actually happened?

Everything you say is made up. Your whole life . . .

I rolled up into a sitting position. I held my head in my hands and groaned.

It was then that the despair rose up inside me with its true face. That laziness, that heavy sadness, that sleepy passivity, waiting for the next thing to happen: the hopelessness had crept up on me like that—had worked its way inside me like a spy, like one of those spies that gets into a city and opens the gates for the enemy army to come charging in.

And now it was here in full force—a horrible feeling, a twisting, hollow anguish of despair.

I took my hands off my head. I clasped them in front of my mouth. I wanted to pray. I tried. But I couldn't. I couldn't even do that because I was too afraid. That accusing whisper spoke to me:

What if it's true? What if your whole life is a lie?

And I was afraid because I realized I might be a murderer. I might *deserve* everything that was happening to me. I might *deserve* to go to prison until I was old. What if I prayed to God and God condemned me? Like the sheriff did. Like Detective Rose did. Like everyone.

I was afraid to pray, but I had to do something and that was all I could think of. I pressed my clasped hands hard against my mouth. I bit into them. I forced the words into my mind.

Please. God. Help me. I'm beaten. I admit it. I'm lost. I've got nothing left. Please. Help.

But no help came.

Instead, a moment later, the Plexiglas door of the cell opened again. I looked up and there was the deputy filling the entrance, his granite face set hard and unsmiling. He had a large plastic bag in his hand. He tossed it at me. My clothes—the clothes Mrs. Simmons had given me—were inside.

"Get dressed, kid," he said. "It's time to go."

Now the river of events started up again, and I was drifting along on it helplessly. I changed back into my street clothes while the deputy stood over me, watching. Then he turned me around and pulled my hands behind my back. I felt the handcuffs snap over my wrists again.

The deputy took me down the hall and back into the big room with the gunmetal desks. There was Detective Rose, waiting for me, his face hard and unsmiling like the deputy's. Behind him were four state police troopers. Their faces were hard and unsmiling too.

The granite-faced deputy handed me over to Detective Rose. He let go of my elbow and Detective Rose took hold of it. It was as if they were passing a package, one to the other.

Now Detective Rose led me to the door. Two of the state troopers went ahead of us. Two more went behind. There was nothing I could do but go with them, carried along on the river of events, my hands locked behind my back by the handcuffs.

We went quickly down another corridor, then out into an anteroom. There were two big wooden doors ahead of us. The leading troopers pushed the doors open. Detective Rose led me through them. We stepped out of the building, into the outdoors.

Everything then was whirling confusion, sensations bombarding me so fast I couldn't make sense of them. People were shouting. There were faces all around me. There were reporters and cameramen jostling one another, trying to get a picture of me, trying to get me to turn their way.

"Charlie!"

"Charlie, look here!"

"Charlie, how did you stay free so long?"

"Charlie—hey, where did you hide out?"

My gaze went from voice to voice, catching glimpses of the scene around me. I saw a shouting woman with a microphone. I saw my own face reflected in the lens of a camera. I saw a crowd—a crowd of frowning faces—

watching me. They were people from the town, people who'd gathered to see the bad guy taken away to jail. The troopers ahead of me pushed the people back, forcing a way for me across the sidewalk.

All of this was mixed up with the brightness of the morning sun as it touched the tops of stores along the street and glared in their storefront windows. It was mixed up with the sweetness of the open air and the terrible frantic desire inside me to drink in this single moment of being in the world because I knew I would never be in the world again. Not for twenty-five years or more. In all that time, I would never see the sun as a free man, never take a walk in the park or go fishing or take a girl to the movies. Twenty-five years to life in prison. My eyes sought out the sun. My lungs sucked in the air.

There was a patrol car in front of me, I saw now. It was parked right in front of me at the curb. A trooper was pulling the rear door open. Now he was holding it open, waiting for me.

Hungrily my eyes went over the scene again, trying to drink it in, make it last, my final moments in the free world. Faces, cameras, microphones, the sun, the street, the sky.

"Charlie—look over here!"

"What tripped you up in the end, Charlie?"

"How do you feel about going back to prison?"

Then two things happened, very quickly, one right after the other.

As I turned my confused gaze this way and that over the scene, I saw a face go past, one of the faces in the crowd. I just caught a glimpse of it. It was the face of a good-looking young man with thick blond hair that flopped down on his forehead. My eyes passed over him and I felt a kind of jolt inside me. It was a jolt of recognition. I didn't remember ever seeing that young man before, and yet all the same I thought to myself: *I know him!*

My eyes went back to find his face in the crowd again. But he was gone. Or at least I couldn't find him among all the other faces, and the cameras and the microphones and the shouting voices.

We were almost at the cruiser now, almost at the open door. The lead troopers were clearing the last couple of yards, pushing the people back to make a way. There wasn't much time. I scanned the faces desperately, but the face I'd recognized was gone.

Then it was too late. We had reached the car. The troopers were gathered around me, keeping back the crowds. Someone was putting his hand on the back of my head to guide it in through the door.

That's when the second thing happened.

Someone—I didn't see who—pressed in very close behind me. I felt a quick, painful pinch on my hand-cuffed wrists. At the exact same moment, I heard a man's voice, very low, whisper right into my ear.

It said: "You're a better man than you know. Find Waterman."

I tried to turn, to see who had spoken, but the next moment, I was pushed down into the backseat of the car. The door slammed shut. I looked out the window, but I couldn't see anything except a wall of khaki uni-forms as the troopers crowded against the car. When I turned to face forward, I was staring at a security grate between me and the front seat. Through the grate, I could see the driver at the wheel, another state trooper. Then the front passenger door of the cruiser opened, and Detective Rose got in and sat down next to the driver.

"Let's move," he said.

The cruiser's siren let out a quick blooping noise and the car started forward.

As it did, I felt my hands shift strangely behind me and I realized: my handcuffs were sliding open.

Somehow, someone had broken the lock.

CHAPTER TWENTY-TWO

Radio News

The jail was in the city of Centerville. I stared through the window as it slipped past. We went along a row of shops. We went down a shadowed corridor of office buildings. I saw a green sign for the interstate go by. Then we were on the highway, gathering speed, and the blue sky was opening before us and the skyline was falling away behind us as the cruiser sped north.

I watched all of this, but barely noticed any of it. I was still dazed from what had just happened. My heart was going a million miles a minute. My thoughts were going just about as fast.

I worked my hands behind my back. I found that I could slide the handcuffs open and closed without any effort at all. Someone—the same man who had whispered to me, I guess—had somehow stripped the lock on them. That must've been the pinch I felt on my wrists. That must've been when he did it. Just before he said those words to me:

You're a better man than you know. Find Waterman.

What did it mean? What *could* it mean? Waterman. I didn't know anyone by that name. But then, I didn't know much of anything anymore. I wasn't even sure I really knew myself.

Still, the words burned like a flame inside me, like a small flame in the roiling darkness.

You're a better man than you know.

Did that mean I wasn't a killer? Did that mean my whole life wasn't a lie, as Detective Rose had said? But who had said that? Who had freed my hands? A friend? An enemy? Someone who knew the truth or someone with a reason to lie?

The cruiser raced along the highway. The thoughts raced through my head, coming so fast they seemed to jumble together. Outside, vast stretches of forest went past, a sea of leaves rising and falling on the hills like waves. The leaves were changing color. Their reds and yellows mixed with the evergreens against the bright blue of the October sky. I stared out at them, but I barely saw them. I worked the handcuffs behind me, opening and closing them.

You're a better man than you know. Find Waterman.

Waterman. Who was he? How could I find him? Was he another part of my life that was lost? Was it gone forever? Might there still be a trace of memory, a clue buried in my mind that I was overlooking?

Again—obsessively—I went back over the events of yesterday, trying to force some fresh detail to the surface of my consciousness. The torture room. The faces of my tormentors. The voices I'd heard outside the door.

Homelander One.

We'll never get another shot at Yarrow.

Two more days.

We'll send Orton. He knows the bridge as well as West.

There was more. There were names. The voices mentioned names. I strained to find them, but I couldn't. I just remembered that one voice saying, *Whatever the truth is, the West boy is useless to us now. Kill him.*

I let out a sighing breath in frustration. It was all crowding together in my mind. The things I remembered, the things that had slipped away, a useless mess of half-understood words and images. What did I know? What was I supposed to believe? What was I supposed to do now?

Find Waterman.

I worked the handcuffs, opening and closing them—and the answer came to me.

I was supposed to escape. Of course. That must be it. That must be what the man had meant when he whispered to me.

You're a better man than you know.

He must've been telling me that I wasn't a criminal, that I should make a break for it and "find Waterman," whoever he was—or whatever.

I looked around the backseat of the car. It was really just a moving cell. There were no handles on the doors. No locks I could open. Even if I took my handcuffs off in here, there'd still be no way I could get out. I would have to wait, look for a chance. I would pretend the handcuffs were still locked until I saw the right moment.

But then what? Once I got out of the car, I would be surrounded by police. Handcuffed or not, I would never be able to get away . . .

I shook my head. Too many thoughts, too many questions. I was beginning to feel overwhelmed. I needed to calm down and stay calm. I needed to think. I needed to make a plan.

That sleepy sadness I had felt in the cell—that passivity and despair—they were gone suddenly. I had hope again. I was thinking again. Trying to take control of things, trying to find a way out.

I remembered how I prayed for help in my cell. How I'd thought there'd been no answer. I was wrong.

Now I had a chance. All I had to do was figure out how to use it.

"Hey, Detective Rose," I said.

Detective Rose hardly glanced back at me. He grunted.

"Are we going straight to the prison?" I asked.

It took him a while to answer. I could tell he didn't want to. He didn't want to talk to me at all.

Finally, though, in a kind of grim, slow voice, he said, "No. Winchester. State Corrections sends a van to the jail there in the morning. They'll take you up to the prison."

"Winchester," I said. "How far is that?"

Detective Rose snorted. "What do you care? You're in no hurry. You got all the time in the world."

The driver gave a heavy laugh. "Twenty-five years, at least."

"Right," I said. "I was just wondering. You know, how long a drive it was."

Detective Rose gave a shrug. "Not long. We'll be there soon. Now shut up. I can't hear the radio."

"The radio's not on."

He turned on the radio. A strain of country music played very low. It barely reached me in the backseat.

I sat back, thinking. If I was going to escape, I would have to do it before they put me in another cell. Once we reached Winchester, once they saw that my handcuffs were loose, I would lose the advantage of surprise. I had to find a moment to break away before we reached Winchester.

"When will I be able to call my parents?" I asked.

Detective Rose turned and glowered at me. "Hey, is my memory going or didn't I just tell you to shut up?"

I pushed on. "I mean, those cameramen outside the jail. I'm gonna be on TV. My mom and dad'll be worried about me."

"You probably should've thought of that before you committed murder."

"Have you seen them? My parents. I mean, you work in Spring Hill . . ."

"Your parents don't live in Spring Hill anymore," said Detective Rose.

I felt my stomach twist a little at that. I remembered how I'd tried to call home at Mrs. Simmons's house. I remembered the recording: *This number has been disconnected.* Now I knew: my mom and dad had moved away. My home was gone.

"Where do they live now?" I asked.

"How would I know?" said Detective Rose. "What am I, a phone book?"

With that, he turned the radio up louder, as if to drown me out. I could hear it more clearly now. The music had ended, and an ad for mattresses had come on. When the ad ended, the news began.

"Winchester County is preparing security for the arrival of the secretary of homeland security on Saturday," the newsman said. "Richard Yarrow will meet with President Spender at his vacation retreat in the Green Hills. The dynamic new secretary, who has completely reorganized the Homeland Security Department, says he and the president plan to discuss what he called a 'bold and uncompromising new program' to fight Islamo-fascist terrorism at home."

I sat up straight, listening intently. The newsman stopped talking and the secretary of homeland security came on.

"The president and I are both strongly committed to rooting out the evil of religious extremism, and we will destroy the specter of terrorism that has arisen in the Middle East and is threatening this nation at home. Our country was founded on the principle that people should be free to worship God as their conscience guides them. We will protect that freedom from anyone who wants to destroy it."

Then the newsman came back with another story: "A fire at the Brandon factory just outside Winchester injured seven people yesterday after a boiler exploded . . ."

His voice faded into the background of my thoughts. I was still sitting up straight in the backseat. Staring into space. Seeing nothing.

Secretary of Homeland Security Richard Yarrow. That's what the newsman had said. And I remembered those voices speaking outside the torture room:

We'll never get another shot at Yarrow.

Secretary of Homeland Security Richard Yarrow was arriving to meet with the president at his vacation home on Saturday.

Two more days.

"We will destroy the specter of terrorism," Yarrow had said. He and the president were discussing "a bold, new initiative" to fight the terrorists. On Saturday . . .

Two more days.

We'll never get another shot at Yarrow.

"They're going to kill him," I whispered.

I hadn't even meant to speak aloud. The words just broke out of me almost before I could think them. And yet the minute I spoke, I knew it was true. I could feel it. It made sense of everything. The people in the compound, the people who had captured me, tortured me, hunted me through the forest—they were terrorists. That had to be it. I don't know how I'd gotten involved with them or what they wanted from me, but I felt sure now of what they were planning. They were going to kill the secretary of homeland security, to derail his new initiative against them.

My eyes focused on the seat ahead of me. The grate holding me. The two men up front, the backs of their heads.

"Two more days," they'd said.

Saturday.

Only one more day now. Saturday was tomorrow.

We'll never get another shot at Yarrow.

One more day and they would assassinate the secretary of homeland security.

I stared at the back of Detective Rose's head as the cruiser sped along the highway.

How could I explain it to him? How could I ever get him to believe me?

CHAPTER TWENTY-THREE
Seconds

I had to try.

"Detective Rose . . . " I said.

Detective Rose shifted in the front seat, twisting around to look at me. I could see those sharp, cold eyes of his staring through the diamond spaces in the grate.

"Listen, West," he said. He had to talk loudly so I could hear him over the radio. "I know you're not stupid, right? You had an excellent grade point average in high school before you left all that behind and began your illustrious career as a murdering piece of garbage. So I know you got some brains in you."

"Detective Rose, listen . . . " I said.

"So when I say something to you, I expect you to understand me."

"Detective . . ."

"And I'm saying something to you now. I'm saying to you: shut up. Is that unclear somehow? Well, let me explain myself further. Shut up or I'm gonna slug you. Got it?"

The driver gave another heavy chuckle.

"You want me to spell it for you too?" asked Detective Rose.

"They're going to kill Richard Yarrow," I said. "The guy they were talking about on the radio. The secretary of homeland security. They're going to assassinate him."

Detective Rose looked at the driver. The driver glanced over at him. I could see Detective Rose's unpleasant, humorless smile through the grate. He reached over and turned off the radio. He turned those eyes on me again.

"What?" he said.

"They're going to . . ."

"Who? Who's going to kill the secretary of homeland security?"

"The men. The men in the woods."

"Oh yeah," said Detective Rose. His round face went up and down as he nodded. "The little men in the woods. I almost forgot about them. Well, relax, Charlie. Maybe they won't kill him. Maybe they'll just carry him off to their magic tree and bake him some cookies."

This time, the driver laughed louder.

"It's true!" I said. "You have to believe me. It's all true. Where do you think I got these bruises, these burns? They captured me. I don't know why. I can't explain it. I can't explain anything. I just know I woke up there and heard them talking. They said they'd never get another shot at Yarrow. They said two more days. That's when Yarrow's coming to meet the president. Don't you see? They must be terrorists. They must be planning to kill him."

Now Detective Rose turned to the driver. "What did I tell you?" he said.

The driver shook his head. "Amazing."

"He's good, isn't he? He's a good liar. I can almost forgive myself for believing him the first time."

I saw a TV show once where this evil doctor declared this guy insane in order to have him locked up in a mental hospital. The guy tried to tell everyone he was sane, but because he was in a mental hospital, no one would believe him. They just thought he was saying he was sane because he was crazy. The guy got so frustrated trying to explain that he was sane that he nearly went crazy . . .

That's pretty much what I felt like now.

I threw my head back against the seat, thumping it. I closed my eyes, trying to fight down my feeling of helplessness. What was I going to do? If I couldn't convince him, Secretary Yarrow would die. I would spend the next twenty-four hours locked away, knowing what was going to happen, powerless to stop it. I couldn't. I had to do something. Get away. Warn someone.

Find Waterman . . .

Something . . .

"Here," said Detective Rose.

I felt the car glide over to the right. I opened my eyes. I looked out the window. There was a sign up ahead on the freeway. WINCHESTER: NEXT FOUR EXITS.

"We're here already?" I said.

"Yeah, too bad," said Detective Rose. "I was so enjoying our little chat."

My heart started racing again. Here we were in Winchester already and I hadn't come up with a plan. I had no idea how I would try to escape. Soon the chance would be past. I had to think of something.

I pressed my face to the window and looked out. I saw a long street with no people in it. Grim warehouses and abandoned brick buildings loomed on either side. I saw garbage in the gutter and paper blowing along the sidewalk. When I turned and looked through the windshield, I could see smokestacks rising up ahead.

The cruiser turned a corner. There was another street, not much different from the last. Old buildings with broken windows. Empty lots littered with papers and metal and cans. Three old men were gathered around a garbage can. There was fire coming out of the can, and the men were holding their hands out to the flames to warm their fingers. I could tell by their scraggly beards and their torn clothes that the men were homeless. They lifted their hollow eyes to watch the cruiser driving past.

Now, when I looked up ahead, I could see one building standing out from the others. The building looked new and shiny, a bright box of metal and glass in the midst of all that dull, dirty brick and cement.

"Is that it?" I said. "Is that the jail?"

No one answered, but I knew it was. We were only a block away. I was running out of time.

I scanned the distance, trying to see what was waiting for me up ahead. I wondered if it would be the same as it was outside the jail in Centerville. Would there be reporters? Crowds? Dozens of policemen? As far as I could see, the street looked quiet. The only person I saw was another homeless man shuffling by a deserted lot.

Detective Rose took out his cell phone. He muttered into it. I couldn't hear what he said, but I figured he was telling the jail we were coming in.

Now the shiny metal-and-glass building was rising up over us on the left as we came near. There was a broad flight of stairs leading up to the line of glass doors at the entrance. I still couldn't see any crowds or reporters anywhere. There were a lot of police cars parked out front, but most of them seemed to be empty. A patrolman did get out of one cruiser, but he trotted up the stairs and went inside without even glancing our way.

"There don't seem to be as many people here as there were back in Centerville," I said. I was trying to find out what to expect.

"Too bad," said Detective Rose. "I guess your fifteen minutes of fame are over. You were just a little break between some pop star going into rehab and some movie actor committing suicide. The news cycle cycles on and you're forgotten."

He sounded like he was taunting me, like he thought

I'd be sorry that I wasn't in the news anymore. But I wasn't sorry at all. The fewer people there were around, the more chance I'd have of making a break for it. Even as it was, the odds were heavily against me. I figured when the time came, I'd have only seconds to make my move before I was taken inside that building, seconds before they discovered my loose handcuffs and put me in another cell.

I could feel the fear of that moment rising in me now, an agony of suspense that flowed through me like a low and growing current of electricity. The cruiser was passing the jail on the left, moving along the base of the steps, past the row of police cars parked out front. Now the driver put on his turn signal. I saw there was an alley right next to the jail, a narrow corridor between the jail's shiny metal wall and the blackened concrete of the parking garage next door.

The cruiser turned and went into the alley shadows. I struggled to slide forward on the seat, to lean toward the grate and look through it, through the windshield at what was waiting up ahead. The alley was empty and, at first, the side wall of the jail seemed solid, an unbroken band of metal at the lower two stories, with grated windows on the six or seven stories above. But as the cruiser continued on, I saw a break in the metal wall, and a heavy door began swinging open. A guard stepped out. He stood in the alley, waiting for us. That's all there was. One guard. Just one.

Inside me now, the current of electric suspense grew stronger and stronger until my nerves were all snap and spark and motion. This was it. My one chance. No time to make a plan. I was just going to have to look for an opportunity and seize it. Seconds to decide, seconds to move.

The cruiser pulled up outside the open door. The driver turned to look at Detective Rose.

"You gonna need a hand?" he asked.

Detective Rose wagged his head as if he was trying to decide. Then he said, "Yeah, just help me get him inside, then you can head back."

"Sure thing," said the driver.

The cruiser's front doors cracked open on both sides and both men got out of the car at once. Detective Rose walked around the cruiser's trunk to come around to my door. The driver—a short, solid-looking man with a rough face and graying hair—simply stood up out of the driver's seat and waited there, leaning on the open door with one hand.

Now Detective Rose was outside my window. Now he was opening my door. I told myself to relax, get ready, take deep breaths. But I was so tense, so anxious, so electric, I could barely breathe at all.

Detective Rose reached into the cruiser and took my elbow. I had to keep my fingers wrapped around my handcuffs to make sure they didn't slip off my wrists and give me away.

"Watch your head," said Detective Rose.

I bowed my head down to clear the door and stood up out of the cruiser.

We were only about three steps away from the jail door. In seconds, I would be inside, my one chance would be over. Seconds . . .

But the seconds seemed long—weirdly long, as if they were passing in slow motion. I guess I was so scared now, so wired up, that my brain was working at a quicker speed. I seemed to have time to look around, to notice everything that was happening. Everything seemed to be sharp and bright, to stand out from the world like the pictures in those pop-up books I used to have when I was little. There was the guard waiting for me at the door. Detective Rose with his face set forward. The driver reaching for my other elbow while his other hand moved to close the driver's door. I caught a glimpse of the cruiser's dashboard: the keys in the ignition.

I moved. Like a magician performing a trick, I ripped my hands free of the cuffs. As the driver reached for my elbow, my hand shot up and eluded his grasp. I grabbed him by the front of his shirt. He was thickset, but I had so much adrenaline pumping through me that I think I could've lifted him over my head and hurled him to the end of the alley. Instead, I just yanked him across my body and shoved him into Detective Rose.

The two men collided. Caught completely by surprise, Detective Rose was knocked off balance. He lost his hold on my elbow and grabbed hold of the driver to keep from falling over. The two men were carried several steps away from me, clutching each other for balance. At the same moment, I grabbed the cruiser's still-open door and jumped inside behind the wheel.

It happened fast, really fast. The guard standing by the jailhouse door didn't even have time to react. I caught a glimpse of his face as I pulled the cruiser's door shut. It was blank—there was no expression on it—as if he hadn't even realized what he'd just seen.

I grabbed the car key and twisted it, jamming my foot down on the gas. As the engine roared to life, I grabbed the transmission stick, threw it into reverse.

Someone shouted: "Hey!" I saw Detective Rose

scrambling to his feet. I saw the driver pushing away from him, reaching for the gun in his hip holster.

But then I was looking away, looking back over my shoulder as, with a screech of rubber on road, the cruiser ripped away from them, shot backward up the alley toward the street.

As I busted out of the alley shadows into the light, I had a horrible shock. The face of a homeless man frozen in a gasp of surprise was inches away from my window. He was just about to cross the alley. If he'd taken one more step, I would have run him right over. But he pulled up short. He shouted a curse. I rocketed past him, took my foot off the pedal, and twisted the wheel, hard.

The cruiser gave another rubber scream and swung around in the street, throwing up a cloud of dust. A horn blasted loudly as a delivery truck nearly crashed into me, swerving away from me in the nick of time.

Even as the cruiser was turning, I grabbed the transmission and knocked it into drive. I caught a glimpse of the alley. Detective Rose was on his feet now, reaching to his belt for his gun. The driver had his gun out already. He was pointing it right at me. He might have had a shot at me, but he didn't take it. Of course he didn't. He was a policeman—one of the good guys. They don't just open fire on someone who isn't going to shoot back.

In the next moment, anyway, his chance was gone. I jammed my foot down on the gas pedal. The cruiser bucked like a bronco and then shot past the alley, heading down the street at high speed.

CHAPTER TWENTY-FOUR

Shelter

There was a TV hanging on the cafeteria wall. A pretty blonde newswoman was on the screen, sitting at a desk, telling the news. She was talking about the arrival of Secretary Yarrow on Saturday. Yarrow had personal ties to the governor, she said, and was stopping off in Centerville to meet him. From there, it was easier for him to travel to the president's vacation home along the highway rather than by helicopter. And because of that, the security precautions were going to tie up traffic in the area. There was a map behind her showing the secretary's route from Centerville to the president's vacation home.

Saturday. Tomorrow. And no one knew the secretary was going to be assassinated. No one but me.

I was in a homeless shelter. It was dark now. Night had fallen. I had been on the run all day—a long, long day . . .

I had ditched the stolen police cruiser as soon as I put some distance between me and the jail. The car was just too easy to spot. The police would have found me in minutes. Instead, after driving a few zigzagging blocks, I jumped out and made my way on foot. I crossed empty lots and ducked down dirty side streets, hoping to hide my trail before the police could get moving and come after me. Finally, I spotted an abandoned brownstone and went inside to hide. On the third floor, there was an open space where there had once been walls and rooms. All that was there now was broken glass and stone and dirt, cold air drifting through broken windows—oh yeah, and rats, big fat ones, nosing around the walls, looking for scraps of food.

I stayed there and listened. Soon the sirens started, one and then more and then more as the police turned out in force to search for me. After a while, there was a helicopter too. I heard its blades chopping the air as the pilot scanned the area below. I sat in the abandoned building and waited. I didn't know what else to do. I thought they would turn out with dogs soon, and then they'd be sure to find me. But the hours went on and I heard more sirens but no dogs. And no one came to the building.

So there I stayed, hour after hour. Waiting, listening, afraid. I slept sometimes, but mostly I just sat—sat and thought about things, trying to figure out what I should do next.

It wasn't an easy thing to figure. I mean, here I was, on the run again just like yesterday—only now it was much, much worse. Yesterday, I thought only the bad guys were after me. I thought all I had to do was find my way back to civilization and call my parents or the police and everything would be fine. Now I realized the police—the good guys—were after me too. My parents had moved away. I was suspected of killing my best friend. Everyone was against me.

Well, no, wait—not everyone. There was that guy— that guy who'd whispered to me as they lowered me into the police car, who had broken my handcuffs and said I was a better man than I knew. He was on my side, who-ever he was. If I could find him, or find this Waterman he was talking about, maybe one of them would help me.

Meanwhile, though, I had another problem, a new problem, a big one. Richard Yarrow, the secretary of homeland security, the man in charge of protecting the country from terrorism. With me a fugitive and the police figuring me for a murderer and a liar, how was I ever going to convince anyone that his life was in danger?

So I sat in that empty room and thought about all this, hour after hour, hugging myself and shivering as the afternoon wore on and the autumn air got colder and blew harder from one broken window to another. After a while, the howls of the police sirens began to fade, first one, then the next, until they were all gone. The helicopter moved away, the chop of its propellers growing softer and softer until I couldn't hear it anymore. By the time the sun went down and the light at the windows faded, it was quiet all around me.

Darkness came, and I edged over to a broken window. I poked my head around the frame and peeked out at the street three stories below. It seemed empty down there except for the occasional homeless guy shuffling along in the dark.

I was hungry now, wondering how I was going to find a meal. I had no money. I hated to think of stealing something, but I knew I had to eat if I was going to go on.

Finally, I left the brownstone. I went down into the street and stepped out into the chilly evening. It was a weird, kind of naked feeling being outside again. I knew my escape must be on the TV news. I knew they must be talking about me and showing my picture and all that. Maybe they were even offering a reward—you know, for information leading to my arrest. I felt as if my face were a neon wanted poster, a big lighted sign saying: IF YOU SEE THIS MAN, CALL THE POLICE.

Stuffing my hands in my pockets and hunching my shoulders against the cold, I moved down the street. I kept looking around to see if anyone noticed me. Every time a car went by, I pulled up, worried it might be a cop. Once, a police cruiser actually crossed my path, heading down an intersecting street. I edged close to the wall of a building, where the darker shadows hid me until the cruiser had gone past.

I had an idea now. Back home—back in my real life when I was just a regular kid—my church had worked with a homeless shelter. Once a month, people from our congregation would go over there and bring food and cook dinner for anyone who wanted it. Sometimes I was one of the volunteers. The homeless shelter was connected to another church, and I knew that a lot of churches in bad neighborhoods like this one ran soup kitchens and shelters to help the poor.

So I looked for a church. Whenever I came to a corner, I lifted my eyes and scanned the area for a steeple or a cross lifted against the night sky. Each time I saw one, I went toward it to see if there might be a soup kitchen, somewhere for the homeless to get something to eat. Somewhere for me to get something to eat.

Sure enough, on the third try, I lowered my eyes from a steeple and saw a line of hunched men standing on the sidewalk. I moved toward them. They were waiting outside a small building next to the church. It was a homeless shelter with a cafeteria. There was a cardboard sign in the window, saying dinner was available at seven o'clock on a first-come-first-served basis. I got in line with the others. When the shelter doors opened, we began to shuffle inside.

I was glad to get in. I was weak with cold by that time. The building was warm, and the warmth slowly sank into me. I followed the others down a little hall that led into the cafeteria. It was a big room, clean and brightly lit, with long tables covered with paper tablecloths. I smiled kind of sadly to myself when I saw it. It reminded me of the cafeteria at school. I never thought I'd miss *that* place. But I missed it now.

I got a tray and stood in the food line at the long counter. I was younger than most of the others there, but we all looked pretty much the same: stooped and un-shaven, with worn-out clothes and dark circles of exhaustion under our eyes. The people behind the counter scooped mashed potatoes and roast beef onto our plates—big heaps of them. They all smiled brightly and said hello to each of us as we went past. It was funny in a way. They acted just like the people from my church acted when they volunteered at the homeless shelter once a month. They acted just like I acted when I volunteered. I remembered all those tired, heavy, unshaven faces going past me as I put the food on their plates. I remembered their exhausted eyes looking at me as they nodded their thanks and shuffled by. It never in this world occurred to me that I would ever be one of them. I guess it never really occurs to anyone.

When my plate was full, I carried my tray to a table. I spotted the TV on the wall and sat where I could watch it while I ate. The news was on—I figured I'd find out if they were talking about me. And of course they were. First there was that story I mentioned about Richard Yarrow's visit, about the security and the traffic and the map of his route and all that. Then, as I sat there watching, a great big picture of me—of my face—appeared behind the newswoman, right where the map had been.

"A fugitive killer arrested yesterday by police has broken free again. Jack Alexander has the latest."

Instinctively, I slouched down in my chair and kind of hunched up my shoulders to keep from being noticed. I glanced around the room to see if anyone had recognized me. It didn't seem that anyone had.

Then I looked at the TV again. There it was: the video of me being taken from the Centerville jail to the waiting cruiser. Detective Rose holding my elbow. The crowd of reporters shouting at me, jostling me. The crowd of onlookers, gawking and staring. The police surrounding me, hurrying me to the cruiser. It was weird to see it like that, from the outside, right there on television. It was weird to see my life transformed into a story on the evening news.

"After more than three months on the run, Charles West was brought to justice yesterday," the reporter, Jack Alexander, said over the pictures. "But it didn't last."

Alexander went on to talk about how I'd somehow managed to break free of my handcuffs and run away. There was a picture of Detective Rose, scowling as he walked past reporters without making a comment.

Alexander said the police were baffled about how I broke out of the cuffs. He said the police effort to track me down had been hampered by recent budget cuts that had left them short on manpower and had eliminated their K-9 Corps—their tracking dogs.

Then they want back to the video of me being led out to the cruiser in Centerville. I was wrapped up in the story now. I leaned forward in my chair, staring at the TV. I was trying to see if there was a picture of the man who'd broken my handcuffs. But no, there was just Detective Rose with his hand on my arm and then, just before I reached the car, the state troopers crowded around me, and the picture just became a blur of khaki.

I sat back. Keeping an eye on the television, I got myself a forkful of potatoes. I started to lift it to my mouth—but what I saw next made my hand freeze in midair.

There were my mom and dad. Right there on TV. They were standing outside a house in front of a lot of microphones. My dad had his arm around my mom's shoulders. My mom was holding a tissue to her nose, crying. She was crying so hard that when she tried to speak, she couldn't. It hurt to see her like that. I always hated it when she cried.

"I just want to say . . ." she began, but then the crying overcame her and my dad had to talk instead.

"We just want to ask the police—please, be careful. Don't hurt our boy. He's only eighteen. Please . . ."

And then, as I sat staring up at the TV, my dad had to stop talking, too, just like my mom. I'd never seen my dad cry before, not ever. I have to admit, it made tears come into my eyes as well.

I put my fork down on my plate with a shaking hand. I lowered my face until I could get myself under control.

But the shocks weren't over.

Now the TV reporter said, "West's girlfriend also had a message for the fugitive."

I looked up quickly. My girlfriend? I had a girlfriend?

There on the TV screen—to my utter amazement—was Beth Summers. I couldn't believe it. But it said so, right there in a caption under her face: "Beth Summers, killer's girlfriend."

My mouth fell open. I must've looked like an idiot, sitting there, staring at the screen with a big open mouth. But that was nothing compared to what I felt like inside. I mean, just to see her—Beth—just to see her face again, made me feel a strange ache inside me as if a hand had wrapped itself around my heart and made a fist. The curling honey brown hair framing her smooth face, her blue eyes, and just that sweetness in her expression that

I could never describe . . . How long had it been since I'd seen her? A day? A year I couldn't remember? Or what felt like a hundred years since I looked at the phone number she'd written on my hand and turned off the light in my bedroom and went to sleep?

Beth was sitting in a living room—hers, I guess, though I couldn't remember ever having seen it. There was a reporter—maybe Alexander—sitting across from her. Now and then they would show his face and he would nod sympathetically as Beth spoke.

Beth's eyes were filled with tears, but her voice was steady.

"Is there anything you'd like to tell Charlie right now?" Alexander said, in that syrupy voice reporters use when they want to sound like they care.

Beth nodded and took a deep breath. Then she looked straight at the camera—straight at me. "I'd like to tell him: Charlie, please, turn yourself in. I just don't want you to get hurt or"—she had to swallow down her tears before she could go on—"or killed, you know? If you come back, we'll keep fighting in the courts. I promise. We'll make everyone see that you're innocent, that you'd never murder anybody. And also, I just want you to know: I still believe in you. I still love you."

The breath rushed out of me as if I'd been punched in the stomach. She loved me? Beth was my girlfriend and she loved me? How had that happened? When had it happened? How could I not remember? Had I held her hand? Had I kissed her? Had we taken walks together and told each other what we thought about and what we wanted to do with our lives? Was all that gone, gone out of my memory forever?

When they cut away from Beth to another picture, I wanted to reach out and grab the television and make it stop. I wanted to call to Beth's image on the screen and beg it to stay there just a little longer so I could look at her. I wanted to say: "Don't go. Don't leave me here in this homeless shelter, hunted and alone. Say that you love me again." But she was gone, and the story ended, and the newswoman behind the desk came back to talk about other things.

I felt so bad, so heartsick, I just rested my elbows on the table and put my hands over my face for a long time.

But after a while, I felt something. You ever do that trick, where you stare at the back of a guy's head until he can feel it and it makes him turn around? Well, I felt that. I felt someone looking at me.

I lifted my eyes. I scanned the room. There he was: a

man, watching me. He was one of the homeless guys, a white man in an old army jacket. He was bald and had a silver stubble of beard and a narrow face with sharp features. He was sitting at a table nearby, mopping up the last of his food with a piece of bread. But all the while he was swabbing the bread around on the plate, he wasn't looking down at it. He was staring at me.

He recognized me. I could tell. He must've been watching the TV the same as me. He must've seen my picture. Then I guess he saw me and he knew who I was. At first, I tried to convince myself it didn't matter. I tried to tell myself that he wouldn't go to the police, wouldn't try to collect any reward that might be on offer. I was so tired, see. Tired of running, tired of being afraid. I didn't want to leave the church shelter. I didn't want to leave the warmth or the light or the kindness of the people behind the counter with their smiling faces. I didn't want to leave the television set. I wanted to sit there and wait until another news program came on in case they showed Beth again and my parents. I didn't want to go out into those cold streets where Detective Rose and the other police were searching for me. So I tried to tell myself that it was all right, that I could stay.

But it was no good. The old man kept watching me.

I could almost hear his brain working behind his dull, grayish eyes. I knew that as soon as he could, he'd tell one of the shelter people about me or even find a phone and call the police.

You know who I thought about then? I thought about Alex. Alex Hauser. I thought back to that night we sat together in my mom's car and talked, that night they say I followed him into the park and killed him. He was so sad that night, so sad and angry. He had lost his faith and he had lost his way. I remembered the things I had told him then. Things I had learned from my dad and from church and from Sensei Mike. I told him he had to keep on trying, to trust in the good things and never give in. I told him he had to keep on believing that God was there and that God knew where he was and would help him keep his spirit strong. Alex got angry at me because he said I didn't understand how hard it was. And you know what? He was right. I didn't understand. Not then.

But I understood now. It can be crazy hard. To keep your faith, to keep going. It can be harder than I ever would have imagined. Sometimes things happen to you, really bad things that aren't fair, things that make you feel so terrible you're not even sure who you are anymore or whether you're right or wrong, good or bad.

Sometimes you feel like there's no one to turn to, and you're all alone and so scared you can hardly move and so tired you just want to curl up in a ball and go to sleep forever. I guess that's kind of the way Alex felt that last night I saw him. And that's the way I felt now.

But I guess I had one advantage over Alex. I guess in some way I'd been training for this time my whole life. I'd been training every day, even in simple things, little things. I trained to keep my mind sharp when I went to school. I trained in karate to keep my body and spirit strong. Even when I just went to church, or when I prayed by myself, it was a kind of training: I was training to remember that I was not alone. I was never alone.

Well, training was over now. This was the real deal. I didn't want to get up. I didn't want to leave the warmth of the shelter. I didn't want to start running again in the night and in the cold.

But I had to. I had to.

I grabbed a roll off my plate and stuffed it in my pocket so I'd have something to eat later on. Then I got to my feet.

It was time to go.

CHAPTER TWENTY-FIVE

A Cry in the Night

I walked and walked. I wanted to get lost in the city in the dark. I knew I needed to get out of here, as far away as possible, before the police hunted me down. But without any money, without any help, I couldn't figure out what I could do or where I could go. I thought about finding a phone, calling one of my friends—Josh or Miler or Rick. It would be so good to hear their voices. Maybe I could even call Beth. Maybe she would say those things to me that she said on TV.

I still believe in you. I still love you.

But no. I was a fugitive, a convicted killer. If they helped me, they would get in trouble with the law themselves, they would become accessories to my crimes. I couldn't do that to them. I had to figure this out on my own. I had to figure out another way to escape from here and clear my name and find Waterman and warn Secretary Yarrow about the Homelanders.

I had walked a long time, lost in my thoughts, when I finally stopped and looked around me. I had come into an open area, a street lined with huge, brick warehouses on one side and railroad tracks on the other. It was dark where I was, but there were streetlights not too far off. Under their glow, I could see some boxcars parked a little way down the tracks. I had this crazy thought about how I could sneak inside one of the cars and then, when the train started moving, I could ride it out of the city.

Luckily, before I could do anything that stupid, something distracted me: a short, sharp, high-pitched noise. A cry in the night.

I turned toward the sound, my muscles tensing. My first instinct was to run away. The last thing I needed was to get mixed up in any kind of trouble, anything that might attract the attention of the police.

But as I looked, I saw something I couldn't run away from. Down the street, a figure moved out of the darkness into a circle of lamplight. I could tell it was a woman even though she was hunched over and kind of shapeless in an old black overcoat. She hurried through the glow, her hand out in front of her as if she was groping for something to hold on to. Then she was gone, swallowed in the shadows beyond the lamplight's reach.

I guessed she had been the one to cry out. I could see she was scared. I could see she was running away from something. But I couldn't see what the trouble was.

Then I could.

The next moment, another figure came into view. It was a man this time, large, lumbering. He came running into the light after the woman. His steps were crooked and unsteady. He shouted in a slurred voice, "Come back here!" He shouted again—a foul word—and then his voice dropped into a mutter of curses.

I hoped he would turn around, go away. But he didn't. As I stood there watching him, he hurried after the woman, stumbling headlong out of the lamplight, into the dark.

I couldn't see either of them. Maybe she had gotten

away. But now I heard her cry out again, and his rough voice answered her in a triumphant, guttural growl. He had her.

I hesitated another second. A fight was sure to bring the police. But what was I going to do? Just stand there and let this woman get attacked? There was no way. Not while I had a chance to stop it.

She cried out again. I started running toward her.

A moment later, I was close enough to see them, even in the deep shadows. They were pressed tight against the brick wall of a warehouse. The man had the woman pinned there, one hand on her throat, the other moving roughly over her body. He was big and thick and powerful and he loomed over her. I could see the whites of his eyes and his bared teeth. I could see her eyes too. I could see the terror in them.

I kept running. I was just going to tackle him and take him down, hold him there until she got away.

But he heard my footsteps. He turned and saw me before I reached him. He kept his one hand on the woman's throat, but his other went in and out of his pocket. A blade flashed dully as it caught what little light there was. He had a knife.

I pulled up short. He held the woman against the

wall. He waved the knife in the air and glared at me through the darkness.

"What?" he said roughly, drunkenly. "What do you want? Huh?"

I was out of breath, my heart thumping, but I tried to keep my voice quiet. "Let her go," I said.

He looked me up and down. Then he gave a hard laugh. "You want to die tonight, punk? Get outta here."

The woman made an angry noise. She grabbed at the hand on her throat and tried to pull away. He shoved her back against the wall, throttling her so hard she gagged.

"Hey!" I said. I took a step toward him.

Suddenly, he threw the woman aside—just hurled her away from him so that she stumbled a step, grazed the wall, and toppled to the sidewalk. She lay there, gasping for breath, clutching her throat.

At the same time, the drunk leapt to meet me, slashing at me with the knife. The blade made a vicious diagonal in the air, a stroke meant to cut me open. I was quick enough to dodge back, my arms flying clear, my body bending so that the blade whistled past, missing me by an inch or two.

We faced each other there in the darkness. He waved the knife around threateningly. He grinned. His eyes were bright and gleaming. He was enjoying himself.

He jabbed at me with the knife again. Jabbed and slashed, making me dance backward. He laughed at that. He crooked his hand at me, beckoning.

"What's the matter, punk?" he said. "You afraid? Come and get it. Come on, come on and I'll show you what I . . ."

In the middle of his sentence, I brought my right foot swinging up from the ground in an arc. It's called a crescent kick. Even though you're standing in front of a guy, it comes looping around at him from the side. The drunk didn't see it until it hit him. Then the edge of my foot struck him in the wrist. The impact knocked the knife right out of his hand. The knife hit the brick wall and fell to the sidewalk with a metallic clatter.

The drunk went for the knife, but I was there first. I let the force of my kick carry me forward and brought my foot stomping down on the weapon where it had fallen. At the same time, I grabbed the front of the drunk's shirt with my right hand and drew my left hand back, ready to strike at his eyes or throat.

All the gleam was gone out of those eyes now, and his snarling laughter was gone too. His mouth was open in surprise and his hands were up in fear, and I could feel him shaking, waiting helplessly for me to strike. Yeah, he was a big man when he was roughing up a woman, when he was pulling a knife on an unarmed man. But he was just a bully—a drunk and a bully and a coward.

I shoved him away from me.

"Get out of here," I told him.

For another second, he stood there, staring at me with that same frightened look on his face. Then he frowned—a sulky, little-boy frown as if he were being sent to bed without his supper.

"What about my knife?" he said.

I laughed. You have to laugh. People are nuts sometimes. "Go on," I said. "Don't make me hurt you."

Frowning, sulking, he began to edge away from me. Weakly, he muttered, "Punk. Why couldn't you just mind your own business?"

I didn't even bother to answer. I stood where I was, my foot on the knife. He kept edging away, edging away. He edged into the light again—the circle of light from the streetlamp.

Then, with a last scowl, he turned and slunk off, out of the light into the darkness, and he was gone.

CHAPTER TWENTY-SIX

Crazy Jane

I turned around, looking for the woman. She was gone as well. I figured she'd run off while I was dealing with the drunk. So here I was alone on the street again and still with no idea where to go, or what to do next.

I bent down and picked up the knife the drunk had dropped. I looked at it. It was a crummy old thing, a switchblade, good for nothing but stabbing people. I drew back my arm and hurled it into the night. I heard it give a distant *chuck* as it hit the gravel on the train tracks.

I started walking again along the line of warehouses.

I got about ten steps before a hand shot out of the darkness and grabbed my arm.

I turned. It was the woman, the woman who'd been attacked. She was hiding in a recessed doorway. As she took hold of me, she stepped out, peering up at me intently.

I looked down at her. She was small. Her torn gray overcoat dwarfed her. She had a large, round face with a strangely innocent, even childlike expression. Her cheeks and forehead were covered in grime and red sores. Her brown hair was so filthy it was matted into dreadlocks. She was so dirty I couldn't tell how old she was—not very old, I thought, maybe thirty or something. She had large, almond-shaped green eyes that moved over me quickly and nervously.

Her voice was a low murmur. "I know you," she said. She said it dreamily, in this kind of distant, eerie tone.

I felt my arm go tense in her hand. "Oh yeah?"

She nodded, a quick, squirrel-like motion. Then, glancing this way and that, she said, "Come with me."

She took me to the corner and down a street, then to another corner and down another street. The whole time she was talking to herself—or maybe she was talking to me, I couldn't be sure. She was talking very fast in that dreamy, low murmur, saying stuff like, "Jane knows . . . they sent the knife-man to keep her quiet . . . about the impulses . . . they're electric, you understand . . . mind control . . . but they can't get Jane . . ." She kept hold of my arm, moving along beside me with small, swift steps. She kept her eyes moving, too, scanning this way and that. Once, suddenly, she drew me into the alcove of a warehouse bay and we hid there. "They're coming. They're coming. Jane knows . . . " she murmured. I figured she was crazy. There was nothing to hide from. I didn't hear or see anything to be afraid of, anyway. But the woman said again: "They're coming. Jane knows." And it turned out she was right: a few moments later, some hulking thugs went by, a small gang of them. We waited in the alcove till they were gone.

We walked on, Jane holding my elbow, murmuring the whole way. Finally, we came to an old brick apartment building, its walls practically black with graffiti. Some of the windows were broken, but there were lights on in some of the others. I caught glimpses of shadows moving inside, so I knew the place wasn't deserted.

"They haven't found this . . . my hideaway . . . my secret place . . . they don't know about it . . . the impulses can't come here . . ."

She pushed the front door open. There was no lock. Murmuring crazily, holding on to my arm, she drew me up the stairway. The second floor was destroyed, abandoned, the same as the building I'd hidden in before. But on the third floor there were walls and doors. Some of the doors were shut, and light came out from underneath them. I heard some low music coming from behind one of the others.

We climbed the stairs to the fifth floor. Then she drew me down the hallway to her door. It was locked with a padlock. The woman—Jane—finally let go of my arm in order to fish the key out of her huge overcoat.

"It's the door, that's why," she murmured. "It's special. The electricity can't get through. It's blocked."

She unlocked the padlock and pushed inside. I followed her.

The air in the apartment was dense and gnarly. It smelled bad, like a litter box that hadn't been emptied in a long time. Sure enough, as soon as I stepped over the threshold, I heard cats mewing. Jane pressed a switch. A dim yellow light came on in the ceiling. And there they were: three cats—one black, one orange, one gray. The gray one took an exploratory pass through my legs, then all three of them clustered around Jane's feet. Jane went on murmuring, but she was murmuring to the cats now, her tone more tender than before. She rigged an iron bar across the door as a makeshift lock. She was talking to the cats the whole time. "There they are, safe and sound, my darlings . . . the impulses can't touch them here . . . none of that nasty mind control for my beautiful darlings . . . Jane will protect you . . ."

The cats, meanwhile, wove in and out between her feet, tumbling over one another and meowing. She had to step carefully not to fall over them as she moved away from the door. The cats continued to follow her as she stooped down and turned on a small electric space heater sitting in one corner. Then she moved on into the kitchenette, murmuring to the cats as the cats mewed back at her.

I looked around. The apartment was one room, and it was an unholy mess. The walls were all cracked and chipped. Some of them even had holes broken through the plaster so you could see the beams and wires underneath. There were great big black plastic bags everywhere—in the corners, against the wall, up on a counter in the kitchenette. The bags were stuffed full of what looked like junk as far as I could see: old clothes and broken appliances and cans and bottles and stuff like that.

There was an old dirty mattress lying on the floor and a lamp standing next to it with no lampshade. There was a chair, too, a dirty old canvas chair, set low to the ground like a beach chair.

And then there were the newspapers. They were all over the place. They were everywhere. They were taped to the wall like wallpaper. They covered the floor like a carpet. They were stacked between the plastic bags. They lay littering the bed and the chair. Newspapers on top of newspapers. The place was practically stuffed with them.

I looked over to the kitchenette. There was a microwave oven on the counter in there, and some stacks of food cans and some spotty bowls and glasses. There were no kitchen cabinets, but you could see the marks on the wall where they'd been torn down. There were more newspapers there too—on the wall, on the counter, and on the floor.

Jane stood in the kitchenette with the cats twining around her ankles. She was cranking a can opener around a can of cat food.

"Have to eat to keep your strength . . . for the big fight when they come . . . they sent a knife-man after Jane tonight, my babies . . . but then *he* came . . . mm-hmm . . .

because he knows . . . because they're after him, too, just like Jane . . ."

The cats fell over one another as she spooned some cat food out into a bowl for them and set it on the floor. They took their places around the bowl and ate hungrily.

"Just like Jane . . . mm-hmm. Mm-hmm. You hungry?"

It took me a moment to realize she was talking to me. "Oh," I said. "No. Thank you, ma'am. I'm fine. I ate a little while ago." Even before I finished, she had gone off muttering again, chattering softly in that same dreamy, eerie tone.

She had gone to work opening another can now, a can of soup. She poured it into a bowl and set the bowl in the microwave, chattering softly all the while it cooked. Finally, she brought it out and carried the bowl over to the mattress. Newspapers on the mattress crumpled as she sat down on them. She huddled there, blowing on the soup, still talking softly.

"If they think so, they don't know Jane . . . not me, not Jane . . . electric rays, impulses, connections . . . that's what they know, that's what they think . . . but not Jane . . . Take a seat, Charlie . . . I'm not afraid of them . . . I'm not going to let them in . . . we know, don't we?"

I stood staring at her. She had called me by my name. *Take a seat, Charlie.* Out in the street, when she said, "I know you," she was telling the truth. She had recognized me. She knew who I was.

"Go on, go on," she said. "Take a seat."

I hesitated another moment, unsure what to do. Should I run away? Would she turn me in? Then I just said, "Thank you, ma'am." And I moved to the canvas chair and lowered myself into it. I watched as she lifted the bowl of soup to her lips. She sipped at it noisily, her dreadlocks falling around her face.

"You know my name," I said.

She came out of the soup and murmured, "Charlie West. Mm-hmm. Jane knows. It's in the papers."

She patted the space around herself on the mattress. She found the page she wanted and handed it to me. I took it. FUGITIVE KILLER CAUGHT, said the headline. There was my picture underneath it, right on the front page. I was staring into the camera with wide, frightened eyes. It was a mug shot. They must've taken it when I was arrested for Alex's murder.

"They got ahold of you, didn't they?" the lady said. "They got hold of you and put out the word, oh yes. Electricity, that's how they do it. Impulses. Mind control.

Oh, they can make you believe anything. They put it in the papers and everyone goes along. Jane knows how it works."

I actually smiled a little at that. It felt like I hadn't smiled in a long time, not really. But it was funny: it was obvious that Jane was crazy, but at the same time, what she was saying made a certain amount of sense too.

"You're not afraid of me, then?" I asked her. "You don't think I'm a killer, like the paper says."

"Oh." She gave a laugh and blew on her soup, leaning into it for warmth. "Oh no, Jane knows you're not a killer. Jane knows. It doesn't make sense, does it? If you were a killer, you wouldn't have saved Jane from the knife-man, would you? It doesn't make any sense at all."

I scratched my head at that, wondering. Because again, she was right, wasn't she? It didn't make sense. Maybe I was just as crazy as she was, but, strange as it may sound, the thought kind of touched me. Here I'd been worrying about whether maybe I really was a bad guy—maybe I was a killer like Detective Rose said. But Jane—Crazy Jane—had come up with the answer. If I was a bad guy, I wouldn't have helped her. If I was a killer, I wouldn't be the person I was. I was grateful to Jane for understanding that and for explaining it to me.

I was grateful to her for believing in me—even if she was crazy.

Unfortunately, the next thing I knew she was babbling pure nonsense again. "They try to put those things in my head, you know, make me believe them. With electricity. Impulses. But not Jane. They can't get Jane. That's why they sent the knife-man. Because I won't believe the voices. The impulses don't work on me. I know what they're up to. I know." She lifted the bowl and slurped some more soup from it.

I was confused now. If some of what she said was true, how did I know the rest wasn't? "Uh . . . who sent the knife-man?" I asked her. "Who sends the impulses?"

She looked this way and that, as if she was afraid someone was listening in. Then she leaned toward me and whispered, "The people from the hospital. They're the ones. It's mind control, that's what it is. They say, no, no, no, no, no, no, but . . ." She shook her finger in the air and laughed at that idea. "Jane knows."

I shivered, but I don't think it was because of the cold. In fact, the little space heater was beginning to warm the place up pretty nicely. It was just kind of spooky being here with her, listening to her weaving between craziness and good sense. So many insane things had happened to me in the last couple of days, it was getting hard to tell which was which.

"They're all around, you know," she said.

I licked my dry lips. "Oh yeah?"

"Mm-hmm. The ones from the hospital. Trying to take me back. The ones who are trying to get you. They're everywhere."

I nodded. Again, it was sort of crazy and sort of true at the same time.

"You can't know who to trust," she said.

"That's right. I don't," I told her.

"You don't know how to escape."

"I don't. They're everywhere, looking for me."

"Mm-hmm. Jane knows. Every time you think you've figured out what's what, they change the whole face of things, don't they?"

"Yes!"

"Pretty soon you're not even sure who you are anymore. You're not even sure if their lies are really lies and your truth is really true."

I shook my head. "I just wish I could remember."

"Mm-hmm. Jane knows." She looked at me hard with her big, quick, almond eyes. Her round, innocent face was very serious and intense beneath all the grime. It was as if she felt we had connected with each other, that we were on the same wavelength. It gave me a weird feeling, to understand her, to be in sympathy with her, and to know she was completely mad.

"They want to take away your freedom," she said.

"They do," I said. "They do."

"They want to kill you."

"I know it."

She looked back and forth, this way and that, as if they might burst in on us any minute. "They have plans. Big plans."

"I know! They want to kill Richard Yarrow!"

I don't know why I told her that. It just sort of came out of me. I mean, we were talking and she was describing things so exactly. I just sort of fell into the conversation as if I were chatting with a sane person. Well, why not, you know? I was all alone, after all. I had no one else to share things with. There was just me and Crazy Jane.

"Richard Yarrow," Jane answered in a hushed, awestruck voice. Her green eyes darted back and forth.

I nodded. "He's coming to visit the president tomorrow. They're planning to kill him somehow, and I don't know what to do. Everyone wants to arrest me and no one will believe me."

"They'll never believe you," Jane echoed.

"I know. And I can't just sit by and let Yarrow die."

"Yarrow," she echoed. Then her mouth formed a circle. Her big eyes got bigger still. "O-o-o-oh," she said on a great long breath. "I know Yarrow."

As I sat in the canvas chair, watching, she set her soup bowl aside and came off the mattress. She started to crawl along the floor on her hands and knees, her eyes searching the newspapers lying under her. The newspapers crinkled and crunched as she moved over them. Soon, comically enough, the cats finished eating and came over and joined her. They rubbed up against her flanks. The four of them—the lady and the cats—crawled around the floor on all fours, Jane's eyes scouring the newspapers the whole time. It was one of the strangest things I think I'd ever seen.

Finally, she repeated, "Yarrow." She picked another newspaper page up off the floor. Carrying the page, she crawled back to the mattress with the mewing cats crawling after her. When she'd sat down again, the cats climbed up on her and gathered in her lap. She handed the newspaper page over to me.

153 CLOSED FOR YARROW VISIT, the headline read. There on the paper was a map very similar to the map I'd

seen on TV earlier. It showed Richard Yarrow's route from the airport to the president's vacation home in the Green Hills. Underneath that was a photograph. It showed a whole bunch of state troopers in their khaki uniforms talking to four men in dark suits. The photograph's caption said: "Secret Service agents brief state troopers on security arrangements for Yarrow's 11 a.m. arrival."

I glanced over the news story. The lady sat on the mattress, watching me over the cats and murmuring to herself. The three cats stretched their faces up to her face and rubbed their bodies up against her.

There was nothing much in the newspaper story that I didn't know already. Yarrow had worked out a new plan to root out terrorism in the United States, and he was coming to present the plan to the president. In a recent speech, Yarrow had said that he felt the threat of terrorism here at home was increasing and had to be dealt with harshly.

I was about to hand the newspaper back to the lady when something in it caught my eye. I wasn't sure at first what it was. Something in that photograph of the Secret Service men with the troopers. I kept looking it over and it kept bothering me, but I couldn't tell why.

Then, all at once, I got it. It was the face of one of the

agents—one of the men in the dark suits. I had seen it before. But where?

I stared at the face, trying to remember. It came to me. It was back in Centerville. Back when they were taking me out of the jail to the cruiser. Just before the man came up behind me and whispered to me and broke my handcuffs, I had seen someone, someone in the crowd. I remembered now. I had had a strange feeling, as if I recognized this person, as if I knew him from somewhere.

Now there he was again: one of the Secret Service agents in the photograph. It was the same man, the same handsome face with the same floppy blond hair. Looking at him gave me the same feeling too. I knew him from somewhere. I couldn't quite remember where it was. It was as if his name was right on the edge of my mind and I just couldn't bring it out. The harder I tried to remember, the more it seemed to slip away from me.

They always tell you when you can't remember something, the best thing to do is stop thinking about it. But I couldn't stop thinking about this. It didn't make any sense. Why would I know a Secret Service agent?

It was no good. I couldn't figure it out. I gave up. Once again, I was about to hand the newspaper back to Jane.

Then, just like that, the name came out of me. "Orton," I said aloud.

For once, the lady stopped her murmuring. She went very still. She stared at me as if I had said something bizarre or amazing. "Orton," she repeated.

"The guy in the newspaper," I said. I don't know if I was talking to her or to myself, but it helped me to say it out loud somehow. "The guy in the picture. I think I know him. I think his name is Orton."

Again, she spoke the name back at me, drawing out the syllables in her weird, dreamy way. "Orrrrtooooon."

And with that, those other voices came back to me, my memory of those voices outside the torture room door:

Homelander One.

We'll never get another shot at Yarrow.

Two more days. We can send Orton. He knows the bridge as well as West.

"Orton," I whispered. "That's right. They're sending him to the bridge."

"To the bridge," whispered Crazy Jane, slapping her forehead.

"That's where they're going to do it."

"That's where they're going to kill Yarrow," she said.

"Yes!"

My eyes moved from the photograph back to the map—the map that showed the route of Secretary Yarrow's trip from Centerville to the president's home. Sure enough, there it was, marked clearly on the page: the Indian Canyon Bridge.

"There it is," I said. I handed the page to her, pointing at the map. "There." She took it, looked at it. "Orton is going to kill Yarrow tomorrow right there on that bridge," I told her.

Crazy Jane stared at the paper. Then she let out a little gasp and lifted her eyes to me. The cats mewed and rubbed against her.

"Oh, Charlie," she whispered. "You have to stop him."

CHAPTER TWENTY-SEVEN

Cans

She made a bed for me on the floor: just a pile of newspapers for a pillow, really, and an old rag of a blanket to
pull up over me. She turned off the light and went back
to her mattress. I lay on the floor in the dark nearby.

I was tired—exhausted—but I couldn't sleep for the
longest time. All I could think about was what would
happen tomorrow: the secretary of homeland security
murdered by terrorists on the Indian Canyon Bridge.
And no one knew about it but the killers and me. Me, a

seventeen . . . no, now an eighteen-year-old kid, wanted by the police as a murderous fugitive.

Crazy as she was, Crazy Jane was right: I had to stop it. Somehow I had to warn Yarrow or warn the police or warn somebody. I just had to. But how would I ever get anyone to believe me? I'd already told Detective Rose about it. He thought I was a liar. Everyone else thought I was a murderer. How could I convince them to take me seriously?

Wide-awake, I thought about it a long time. I thought about going back to Centerville to try to warn Yarrow myself. But how would I get there? I didn't have a car. I didn't have any money. I considered hitchhiking—but how long could I stand out there on the open highway before a police car went by or some driver recognized me and called 911 . . . ?

While I was thinking about all this, one of the cats—it was too dark for me to see which one—climbed on top of my chest. Purring loudly, he kneaded me with his forepaws so that I felt the sharp prick of his claws in my flesh. When he was done with that, he curled up on top of me and lay there, purring. I listened to the sound, comforted by the warmth of his furry body . . .

Then a hand grabbed my shoulder. I sat up, terrified

and confused, blinking, looking around. Had the police found me?

No. It was Crazy Jane.

There was a bit of gray light seeping into the room now. I realized I must've fallen asleep. It was almost dawn. In the faint glow of morning, I could see Jane squatting there next to me. Her hand was clutching my shoulder. Her big eyes were gleaming.

"It's all right," she said in a low murmur. "It's too early for them . . . the impulses don't start till the sun comes up . . . We can get the cans before they reach us . . ."

"The cans?" I asked sleepily.

"Come on."

My body ached as I worked my way up off the floor. It was going to be a while before the bruises and sores healed. I followed Jane's shape in the dark room. The sound of her crazy muttering came ceaselessly from her silhouette.

"Jane knows what to do. They can't stop Jane. They can't take Jane back to the hospital. I know it's mind control. I know how they do it. Electricity. That's the secret."

It went on like that as she took me out of the apartment, down the stairs again, back out into the street. A damp, bitter morning chill had settled over the city. It ate through the flannel of my work shirt and brought goose bumps out on my arms. Just as she had before, Jane took hold of my elbow and started walking along in that quick, choppy, squirrelly way of hers. Just as before, she kept talking as she walked.

"Jane knows. Jane knows. They can't fool Jane."

The city was still quiet. Cars went racing by on the all-but-empty streets. The few pedestrians we passed on the sidewalk were still night people, hunched and solitary. They paid no attention to us.

The sky grew steadily brighter as we went, and the traffic grew heavier. But the sun still hadn't come up over the horizon when we stopped on the sidewalk in the warehouse district where we'd met the night before.

We were standing in front of a large, empty lot. It was big, nearly a city block wide and long. Maybe it had been a park once, or maybe there were buildings here and they'd been torn down or fallen down. Whatever the reason, there was nothing here now but an unbroken field of garbage and debris: piles of rubble, rebar, discarded appliances everywhere—and papers and coffee cups and fast-food boxes tumbling through it all, blown by the dawn wind.

Jane let go of my arm. She worked her hand into the

depths of her voluminous coat. When the hand came out again, she was holding two black plastic trash bags—the same kind as the ones lying around all over her apartment.

"Cans," she said, stretching out the word in that strange way of hers. "Caaaaans."

She handed one of the bags to me and walked into the empty lot, carrying the other one.

At first, I couldn't figure out why we were here or what she was doing. I just stood there, shivering in the cold, and watched as Jane moved into the empty lot, wading through the debris and garbage with her quick steps. Her chin was lowered almost to her chest, her head was down as she began to walk from one end of the lot to the other. Once or twice, I heard her murmur softly: "Caaaaans."

Then she picked one up. It had gotten brighter now, and I could see what it was from where I was standing: an aluminum soda can. Of course, then I understood. She was collecting cans so she could get the deposits. I used to do the same thing when I was little. When you buy a soda in our state, you pay a ten-cent deposit on the can. Then when you take the can back, they give you back the dime. It's supposed to stop people from throwing the cans away and making a mess. But of course people are lazy and they throw the cans away anyway. If you go out and look around, you can collect them—a lot of them—enough to make some pretty good money. As always, Crazy Jane was not as crazy as she seemed.

So I joined her. And as the day slowly broke, the two of us moved in concert over the field of garbage. She crossed one way and I crossed the other, searching the ground for cans. In the middle, we would pass each other and I would hear her murmuring, "Jane knows . . . the impulses can't fool her . . . it's mind control, that's all . . . to take me back to the hospital . . . " and other nutty stuff like that. Then I'd go past and she'd go past and we'd go on crisscrossing through the garbage, searching for cans.

There were a lot of them. I guess Jane had some experience in this and knew all the best places to look. By the time the sun finally edged up over the railroad tracks across the street, her large black plastic bag was rattling with cans, and so was mine. By then, too, my back hurt something fierce, and I was tired. This was hard work, moving back and forth, bending over, scanning the ground. And the bag kept getting bulkier and bulkier as I added more and more cans, making it harder to work.

We went on for what felt like a long time, at least an

hour after the sunrise. After a while, I started thinking about that story in the newspaper. It said that Yarrow was arriving at eleven a.m. and would meet with the governor for an hour before traveling to the president's house. That didn't give me a lot of time to get back to Centerville, to find him, to warn him. But I couldn't get back to Centerville without money. So I went on—back and forth across the field, wrestling cans out from the rebar and rubble and stuffing them in my bag.

Finally, Jane stopped. She straightened. She stretched backward, her grimy, pocked face turned up to the morning sky. Her plastic bag sat on the ground beside her, bulging with cans.

"That's all," she said.

I looked around me. We were only about halfway over the field. "That's all?" I said. "Are you sure?"

She nodded. "Jane knows."

Once again, we went off together, she and I, walking down the street side by side, each of us now carrying a bag stuffed full of cans. Jane kept her free hand on my elbow as always and, as always, she kept up her murmuring, guiding me along with her quick steps.

It was full morning now. The city was waking up. There were a lot more people around us. There was traffic on the broad avenues—cars, taxis maneuvering for space, and the occasional bus rumbling by. There were men and women hurrying past us on every side, more and more of them coming out of their apartment buildings, coming out of stores, heading for their cars or bus stops, heading for work. With every step we took, I felt more exposed. Here we were: a young guy and a muttering crazy lady carrying two huge plastic bags full of soda cans. We kind of stood out in the crowd, if you see what I mean. Any minute, I thought, someone would take a good look at us and recognize me. Or maybe a policeman would go by and spot me. Any minute, I thought I was going to have to drop my bag and run for it.

But it didn't happen. Because I think the truth is, in a funny way, we didn't stand out at all, Jane and I. She with her grimy face and her big overcoat and her skin sores, and me with my bleary eyes and my two days' growth of beard: we just looked like two crazy homeless people, wandering the streets with our bags. Instead of staring at us, people looked away from us on purpose. So they wouldn't have to pay attention to us, you know, or think about us or stop and give us money. In a funny way, we were invisible.

All the same, I was glad when we reached the super-market. Whether it made sense or not, it felt safer, somehow, to be inside, off the street. The can-return machines were right near the glass doors. They were two big blue boxes with big round holes in the center of them and digital readouts off to the side. We set our bags down next to them and began reaching in and bringing out the cans, stuffing them into the holes in the machines. We could see the amounts of the deposits mounting up dime by dime on the readouts.

I kept looking over my shoulder, afraid someone would recognize me. But the store was pretty empty, and anyway, like I said, we were just two homeless people bringing in our cans. No one paid us any mind.

Finally, we were done. The digital readout on my machine was $9.50—nearly a hundred cans. Jane beat me, bringing in $12.70. We pressed the buttons marked End, and each machine spit out a receipt. I waited while Jane took the receipts over to the cash register. The lady there paid her the $22.20. Jane took it in her fist and stuffed it down deep into the pocket of her overcoat.

Then she came back to where I was waiting at the machines. She took my arm, murmuring to herself. Murmuring to herself some more, she started walking with her quick steps. I let her take me back out onto the street.

She didn't stop there. She went on walking and talking.

"They shouldn't have tried it. They shouldn't have tried their mind control on Jane. Now Jane knows. Jane is ready for them."

I went along with her, wondering where we were headed. About ten minutes later, I found out.

We came to a busy corner closer to the center of town. There was a food market there and an old, run-down hotel. People were rushing by us on every side, even jostling us sometimes, but none of them paid us any attention. I looked around, trying to figure out why we had stopped. Then I saw the bus station.

It was right across the street, a one-story building with large plate-glass windows. It was set near a parking lot, and the lot was full of buses. I knew there would be one there that would take me back to Centerville. I had a strange feeling in my stomach, sort of like the one you get when an elevator drops too fast.

I turned and looked down at Jane. She was peering up at me with that big round face and those big round eyes of hers. She let go of my elbow and took hold of my wrist. She lifted my hand and brought her fist out of her pocket. She was clutching the twenty-two dollars we'd gotten for our cans. She put the money into my hand.

"No, wait," I said. "Jane. You can't give me all of it. You've got to keep some for yourself, for food and stuff. We both found the cans. We should split the money so you can get something to eat."

But all the while I was talking, she was going on in that dreamy murmur: "No, no, no, no, no, no, no." Pressing the money against my palm, forcing my fingers closed around it.

When she looked up at me again, my eyes went over her—over her filthy, matted dreadlocks and over the patches of dirt on her skin and over the broken sores where red showed through and finally back to those wide, strangely innocent eyes.

"Jane . . . " I said.

"Take the money, Charlie," she said to me. "Take the bus. Stop them. Stop Orton."

"But Jane, listen . . ."

Her long, serious mouth curved upward at one side in a faint hint of a smile. "Don't you worry. They can't get Jane . . . they try and try, but Jane knows. Electricity is the secret. Mind control."

"You have to have money, though . . ."

"Jane is ready for them. Jane goes on." She forced my fist back toward me with the money held tight inside. "Charlie isn't one of them. Charlie stopped the knife-man."

I nodded. "That's right."

"Charlie's my friend."

"That's right," I told her. "I'm your friend, Jane."

She pressed her lips together. Her big eyes filled up with tears. "Take the bus. Stop Orton, Charlie." She gave my fist a final pat and let it go and said, "Think about Jane."

"I will," I told her. "I will."

She turned and started to walk away from me with her quick, clipped steps. For another moment or two, I could hear her murmuring, "Charlie will stop Orton. Charlie stopped the knife-man. Charlie is my friend. Jane knows."

Then, as I stood there watching, she disappeared into the hurrying crowd.

CHAPTER TWENTY-EIGHT

Beth

My mom called me and I woke up, my face pressed deep into the soft pillow. Her voice came again, drifting to me from the bottom of the stairs. I was so tired I didn't want to get up. It was so sweet here, so comfortable and warm under the covers of my bed. But my mom kept calling, and I was desperate to go to her. I wanted so much to see her face again, to hear her voice saying, "Don't get too close to the hot stove. You'll burn yourself." I wanted to see my father reading his newspaper at the breakfast table. I even wanted to hear my sister, Amy, screaming in wild panic over the fact that her new jeans had been left in the washing machine overnight. I'd been away from them all such a long time.

As my mother called to me again, I became afraid—afraid that she would lose her patience and stop waiting for me. I became worried that when I got out of bed and went to the top of the stairs, she would be gone and my father would be gone and Amy, too, and the house would be empty and I would be alone.

It was that fear that woke me up—that fear and the voice of the bus driver coming over the loudspeaker to announce that we had reached Cale's Station, ten miles south of Centerville.

I sat up and looked around. My heart sank as I realized that my mother's voice, my soft pillow, my warm bed—it had all been a dream, just a dream. I was alone again, on the run, here in the cramped seat of this bus heading toward an appointment with an assassin.

The bus came to a stop, and the hydraulics hissed as the door came open. Two or three of the other passengers got up and shuffled down the aisle toward the exit. I slid out of my seat and shuffled after them.

This was my stop, Cale's Station, a small village surrounded by forested hills. I had bought a ticket all the way to Centerville. It had cost me eighteen dollars. With some of the bills I had left, I had bought myself a detailed map of the area. Reading the map on the bus, I had noticed something. If I went the full distance into Centerville, it would be almost impossible for me to get to Indian Canyon Bridge, where I thought Richard Yarrow was going to be murdered. With Highway 153 blocked off for security reasons, there was no other passage to the spot. But the bus traveled on the interstate, which ran almost parallel to 153, separated from it only by the woods. Cale's Station was directly opposite the bridge. If I could get over the hill, I could come down the far side and maybe put myself in the way of Yarrow's motorcade and stop it before it reached the bridge. That would at least be dramatic enough to put the Secret Service on alert. Then, if I could point them to Orton, maybe I could convince them to question him. Or something like that.

It wasn't much of a plan, I guess. Even if it worked, there would be one big drawback to it. Maybe I could stop the motorcade, maybe I could convince the Secret Service that Yarrow was in danger, maybe I could even save the secretary's life—but the police were sure to arrest me. I would be taken back to prison for good. I figured it was possible that my actions in saving Yarrow would be taken into consideration. I had a daydream that the president came to see me and said, *Well, Charlie, my boy, I don't know what all this fuss is about you murdering Alex Hauser, but to thank you for your service, I'm giving you a full pardon.*

Yeah, right. Like that would happen. It'd probably be more like, *Well, Charlie, my boy, thanks for your help. Be sure to look me up in twenty-five years to life when you get out.*

I climbed down off the bus. I shivered as the air hit me. We were up in the hills here. It was colder than the city, and all I had to wear were the jeans and flannel work shirt I'd gotten from Mrs. Simmons.

I found myself standing in front of the Cale's Station bus depot. It was a small box of a building at the very edge of a short, rural main street. I headed for the door. I knew I had to get moving, start hiking over the hill. It was already after eleven. In less than an hour, Richard Yarrow's motorcade would start traveling over the highway toward the canyon bridge. Even if I started right now, I was going to have to hike fast to cut him off.

All the same, before I started, there was one more thing I had to do.

There wasn't much inside the depot. A ticket window with no one behind it. A couple of benches against the wall. An old pay phone.

I went to the phone. Like I said, I figured when this was over, I would be going back to prison. That's if I was lucky. If I wasn't lucky, I might just get myself killed. In either case, I wanted one last chance to say good-bye.

I picked up the handset and pressed zero for the operator, then I dialed the number. It was the number Beth Summers had written on my arm. I had read it over so many times that I knew it by heart. I'd forgotten the whole year of my life that followed that moment, but I remembered the number.

The operator came on. I told her I was placing a collect call to Beth from Charlie. As I waited, listening to the phone ring, I looked over my shoulder to make sure no one recognized me. The place was empty.

"Hello?"

The sound of her voice sent an ache through me. It was the same kind of ache I'd felt on the bus when I woke up and realized my mom wasn't really calling me, that it was just a dream. It was that yearning to be back home again, back in school, talking to my friends and trying to figure out calculus and asking Beth to go to the movies.

It was an ache to be normal and have my life back and have everything be all right.

I opened my mouth to talk to her, but the operator cut me off.

"Will you accept a collect call from Charlie?" she said.

I heard a little sound far away over the line, a little intake of breath. There was a silence after that. Then, in a weak voice, Beth said, "Charlie?"

"Yes, ma'am. Will you accept the charges?"

"Yes. Yes, I will."

I licked my lips. My throat suddenly felt dry, almost too dry for me to speak.

"Charlie?" came Beth's voice over the line.

"Hi, Beth," I said. "It's me."

"Oh . . ." There was another silence, another breath, and when she spoke again I could tell she was crying. "Charlie . . . are you all right? Are you hurt or anything?"

For a minute I couldn't answer. I didn't know what to say. I mean, no—no, I wasn't all right. I was lost and alone and afraid. Everything I loved, everything I knew, was gone. Terrorists were trying to kill me. The police were trying to arrest me. I was setting off to do something that seemed almost impossible, and even if I succeeded I'd probably end up in prison or dead. No. No, I would have to say I was very much not all right.

"Charlie?" said Beth again, crying.

"Yeah. Yeah," I said. "I'm okay, Beth. I'm fine. I just wanted . . . I just wanted to hear your voice. I needed to hear your voice, that's all."

"Charlie, what are you doing? They're hunting for you everywhere. Your picture's on TV. You've got to turn yourself in. You could be shot. You could be killed."

I nodded, but for a second or two I couldn't answer her. Finally, I got the words out. "Listen, Beth. Before I can turn myself in, there's something I have to do. But the thing is, it's kind of dangerous."

"Charlie . . ."

"Listen to me, Beth. You have to listen and you have to tell my mom and dad what I say too. Okay?"

"What? What is it?"

Her voice was so sad, so tearful—there was so much emotion in it—that I wanted to reach out over the distance between us and wrap my arms around her and hold her close and tell her it was going to be all right.

But all I could do was say: "I don't know what's happened. About Alex and everything . . . I always tried to be a good person . . ."

"I know that. Your mom and dad . . . we all know it. We all believe in you, Charlie."

"Whatever you hear about me next, I just want you to know: I was trying to do the right thing. See, there's a man who's going to be killed . . ."

"What? Charlie, what are you talking about?"

I closed my eyes. I leaned my forehead against the cold plastic edge of the phone booth. There wasn't enough time. It was all too complicated to explain. I just wished I could see her. I wished I could touch her face.

"Never mind," I said. "It doesn't matter. I just want you to know that I'm trying to do what's right. There are all these bad things happening. I can't make anyone understand. I don't understand it myself. The thing is, Beth, I can't remember anything. I mean, I remember everything up to that day you gave me your phone number, but after that—this whole last year—it's just gone."

When I stopped talking, I heard Beth crying, sniffling. "You don't remember?"

"This year. What happened. It's all a blank."

"You don't remember . . . us? You and me?"

I reached my hand up to the phone as if I could reach through it and touch her. "I remember you," I said. "I remember you and how much I liked you, but . . ."

"But . . . you said you loved me . . . we love each other. Don't you remember?"

My throat felt so tight I could hardly get the words out. "I want to, Beth. Believe me, I want to a lot, but . . ."

Beth's voice sounded sad and small. "We were going to spend our lives together. You were going to join the Air Force and we were going to get married . . ."

I shut my eyes tight. I was sorry I'd called. It was selfish. I hadn't accomplished anything. I'd just hurt her feelings.

"I want to remember, Beth, I really do," I told her. "I'm trying as hard as I can. Beth, listen, I just have to do this one thing and then . . . somehow, I'll find my life again . . . I'll find you again . . . I promise. I just . . ."

"I love you, Charlie," Beth said.

My heart swelled up in my chest.

"I'll come back to you, Beth," I told her. "So help me, I will find my life again and I will come back to you."

My hand was shaking as I reached out to hang up the phone.

CHAPTER TWENTY-NINE
Death Over Indian Canyon

As I walked down the road, I felt as if there were a lead weight in my chest. I could still hear Beth's voice inside my head. *I love you, Charlie.* I could still hear the sound of her tears.

I thought about that, and I thought about my father crying on TV. And about my mother crying so hard she could barely speak. I'd caused everyone so much pain—so much pain—and I didn't even know how or why.

I walked along the side of the road, leaving the little town of Cale's Station behind me. I'd barely gone half a mile when the road curved. I looked back and saw that the last buildings and houses of the town had disappeared from sight. I waited while a huge tractor trailer went groaning past. Then I was alone.

I left the road and headed up into the forest.

There was no trail. I had to push through underbrush and tangled branches. The going was slow at first. But as I went higher, I found myself in the shadows of tall pines where there was little undergrowth. The ground was more open here, and I could move more easily among the tree trunks.

All the way, the sadness traveled with me. I didn't know if I could stop what was going to happen, but whether I did or not, I was pretty sure I would not escape. At the very least, I was going to be captured, arrested, sent back to prison, maybe for the rest of my life. I couldn't prove my innocence. I couldn't even remember for sure if I was innocent. All those tears I had caused—they were going to keep on falling. I couldn't see any way to a happy ending.

I climbed on. It was cold in the shadows beneath the trees, but the walk warmed me. Soon I was sweating into my shirt. I'd bought a bottle of water at the bus station with my last dollar. I stopped near the top of the hill to take a sip. I checked my watch. It was five minutes after noon. Assuming he was on schedule, Richard Yarrow would be starting his trip from Centerville. Judging by my map, he would be at the Indian Canyon Bridge in about twenty minutes. I had to hurry.

When I reached the crest of the hill, I found a clearing where I could stand and look out at the other hills to the west and north. They spread out in front of me, rising and falling expanses of autumn trees. They looked peaceful from where I was. For a moment or two, the view held me there. I stood and gazed at it without thinking. I would've liked to have remained standing there that way a long time. But I blinked and came back to myself and headed down the hill.

With gravity helping out, the trip down was quicker. I spilled along the side of the mountain, the rocks and dirt tumbling out from beneath my feet. Sometimes I had to grab at trees to keep from falling. It wasn't long at all before I began to sense I was getting close to the road. I still couldn't see it, though—not at first.

Then, suddenly, there it was. The forest ended and gave way to a short expanse of rocky cliffs. Underneath the cliffs was the Indian Canyon Bridge.

The setting was amazing, really majestic. Below me

and to my right, the forest just seemed to open wide. The trees parted on two sheer rock walls that plunged down into a gray stone canyon six or seven hundred feet below. On the far side, you could see the winding highway appearing and disappearing through the gaps in the hills. Finally, it emerged for a last stretch of straightaway and then reached the canyon itself. There it became the graceful arch bridge of gleaming steel, a narrow man-made passage that seemed almost to leap from one side of the gulf to the other. The bridge was at least as long as the gorge was deep, and the steel lacework of the arch structure that held it up looked so light it seemed to float impossibly in the empty space.

The moment I came out over the edge of the rock to see the bridge, I had to drop to my belly so I wouldn't be spotted. The police were already there. I hadn't expected that. Slowly, carefully, I inched my head up over the rock again until I could see them.

There were two state police cruisers, one parked just below me at one end of the bridge, the other stationed at the far end, where Yarrow's motorcade would soon be. Between the two cruisers was another car—dark blue, unmarked—parked in the bridge's center. There was one man standing by each car, a state trooper in khaki beside each cruiser, and a man in a dark suit standing by the unmarked car in the middle.

This was bad, really bad. I glanced at my watch. It was twenty after twelve. By my calculation, Yarrow's motorcade should be coming into view around the final bend in the road any minute. How could I get down to the road, cross the bridge, get in front of Yarrow's motorcade, and stop him before he was attacked—without the police spotting me and arresting me first?

I racked my brain to think of a plan. Obviously, the easiest way to avoid the police would be to work my way to the other side of the bridge through the forest, skirting the canyon. But was there enough time for that? I figured I had no choice but to find out.

But before I could, the killing started.

I was just about to move back into the trees when the man in the blue suit—the Secret Service agent standing by the unmarked car in the middle of the bridge—lifted his hand to his ear. I could tell he was listening to something—a message of some kind coming in over his earpiece. He stood like that a second or two, then he came away from the side of the bridge and stepped out in the middle. He lifted his hand to his mouth. I guessed he was talking into a microphone.

The state troopers at either end of the bridge reacted. They came away from their cars too. They moved to the center of the road, the same as the agent. They were looking at him. He lifted his hand and waved them toward him, first one then the other.

The state troopers hesitated a second. This wasn't what they were expecting. Then they started to come forward, approaching the agent from either side.

A movement in the corner of my eye caught my attention. I turned and saw the first car of the secretary's three-car motorcade appear on the road in a gap between the hills. It didn't look to be that far away. I figured it would reach the bridge in about five minutes, maybe less. That settled it. There was definitely no time for me to make my way through the woods to the other end of the bridge before the cars arrived. I would have to go straight down and warn the police already stationed there. I would just have to hope they believed me and stopped the motorcade. There was no other choice. I was out of time.

I was about to head to the end of the bridge and crawl down onto the pavement where one of the state cruisers was parked. I took one last look and saw the two state troopers now approaching the agent from either end. The agent waited until they were about ten feet away.

Then he went into his jacket and pulled out a gun.

My lips parted. I understood at once. The man in the blue suit: it was Orton.

I was about to shout out a warning. But I had no chance—and I was too far away; they wouldn't have heard me anyway. All I could do was stare as the man in the blue suit pointed his pistol at the state trooper on his far side and fired. There wasn't much noise, only a muffled report. But I saw the hole open in the trooper's chest. He started to fall but before he did, the man in the blue suit turned around and fired again, hitting the second trooper just where he'd hit the first.

The first trooper had fallen to his knees. Now he toppled over onto the surface of the road. The second trooper was staggering backward. Then his legs folded under him and he went down.

As I lay there, gasping, staring, the man in the blue suit—Orton—calmly slipped his pistol back inside his coat. He walked to the unmarked car parked by the side of the bridge. He pointed his key at the car and pressed a button. I heard an electronic chirp. Then the trunk slowly came open.

From my position on the rocks, so far from the center of the bridge, I didn't have a clear view of the trunk's contents. I didn't need one. I could see there was some sort of mechanism in there, and it wasn't hard to guess what it was.

The car was a bomb. Orton was going to wait for the secretary's motorcade, then blow up the bridge and send him and everyone with him crashing to their deaths in the canyon below.

Almost as the thought came to me, I was off the rock, racing to the edge of the bridge. I slid down the last part of the incline and tumbled onto the road. Then I was on my feet, running over the bridge as fast as I could.

There was no more time to think or plan or do the smartest thing or the safest. I had to get to Orton. That was all I knew. I had to reach him—I had to stop him— before he destroyed the bridge and everyone on it.

CHAPTER THIRTY

The Battle for the Bridge

It wasn't far—but it was the longest run of my life.

Orton was at the center of the bridge. He had his back to me. He was leaning over the trunk of his car, working on the mechanism inside—activating the bomb, I guessed. I flew toward him, pumping as hard as I could, knowing that any second he might hear me, might turn and see me and gun me down as he had the troopers.

One of the dead troopers lay between us in a

spreading pool of blood. It was a horrible sight. But I didn't stop. I couldn't. I had to push past it. I had to get to Orton.

I ran and ran. It seemed to take forever. Slowly, slowly, I got closer, closer.

I was only a few steps away when he heard me coming.

He turned to look over his shoulder and spotted me. His mouth dropped open, and his smooth, long features showed his surprise. I didn't slow down. I kept charging at him, full speed. He recovered himself quickly. He jammed his hand into his jacket. He started to draw his pistol again. I could see there wasn't going to be time to reach him before he leveled it at me.

He swung around. He pointed the gun at my chest.

Then I was on him.

I spun to the side. He fired. The bullet went past me. I grabbed his wrist with my left hand, pulling it past my body, pulling him toward me. I hit him with my right fist, sticking the thumb out so it went into his eye.

The blow stunned him. I twisted his gun hand. I grabbed the gun and pulled it free. I stepped away and turned the gun on him.

He kicked it out of my hand.

It was a great kick. A black-belt kick. The kind you usually only see at tournaments, at the highest level. It caught my wrist full force and sent my arm flying upward, the gun spinning out of my hand and into the air.

I never got to see where it fell.

Orton let the force of the kick bring him close to me, spinning to bring a slashing hand around at my throat.

I managed to duck. The hand chopped into the side of my head. It felt like a hammer blow and knocked me to the ground.

I rolled to get away from him. Orton, seeing me on the ground, charged after me. That was a mistake. I looped one foot behind his ankle and kicked out with the other, catching him just below the knee. It toppled him over to the pavement. I leapt on top of him.

The next moment, we were locked together on the bridge, ripping at each other's faces, looking for an opening, each of us trying to drive a knee into the other's groin or ribs. We rolled over each other once and then again, and then I was thrown free and smacked into the bridge's railing, hard. The impact stunned me. Orton seized his chance. He drew up on his knees, drew back his fist, ready to knock me out.

I lashed out with my leg and kicked him in the chest.

He toppled over backward and rolled. I rolled and got to my feet. He was up first and rushed at me.

I was pinned against the bridge's railing. I could feel the top of it where it hit me in the small of the back. Orton was coming in low and fast. I think he wanted to pick me up and lift me over the rail, hurl me down to my death in the canyon. The whole thing happened in a second. He was there. I was spinning aside. His arms were out, reaching for me. I dodged his grip and caught hold of his shirt and his shoulder.

I swung around and hurled him at the railing full force. He hit—and flipped over it.

It happened so fast there was no time to stop it. One moment Orton was at the bridge rail, the next he was spilling across the top. The sight of him tumbling over toward certain death made my heart clutch. Without thinking, I lunged after him, trying to stop his fall.

I touched something. I grabbed it. His arm. His wrist. I had him. His weight pulled me hard against the railing, nearly pulled me over with him. I braced myself against the steel. Held my grip on his wrist. I looked over the railing, looked down.

Orton's face peered up at me, a mask of terror. His body dangled over the abyss. Moment by moment, his weight was dragging him down, dragging him out of my grip. Already, I could feel his arm slipping through my fingers.

"Help me," he said.

I got a better hold on him. It wasn't easy. I had to pull him up until I could reach him with my free hand. Then I had two hands on him. He grabbed hold of my wrist too. But my grip still wasn't very good. I wasn't sure whether I'd be able to pull him up or not.

"Help me, Charlie," he said then.

His words stopped me. I stared down at him where he twisted above the chasm.

"You know me," I said.

"Pull me up, please," he said, his voice straining.

I held on to him, but I didn't try to pull him up. "Who are you?" I said down at him.

Orton glanced down at the fatal fall beneath him. Then he glanced up at me again desperately.

"Please," he said.

"Just tell me. Then I'll pull you up. Who are you? Why are you doing this?"

"You know me, Charlie. I'm Howard Orton. I'm your friend. One of the Homelanders. Just like you."

I stared. "Like me?"

"Please . . ."

"Tell me," I said. "Tell me or I'll let you fall."

I wouldn't have done it, but he didn't know that. He started to talk, babbling in his fear.

"I was always on your side, Charlie. I told them they were wrong about you. I swear. You know Prince. You know what he's like."

I felt him begin to slip from my grasp again. I adjusted my hold to get a better grip, but I was losing him. "I don't know Prince. I don't know you. I don't know any of you. Who are you? Who are the Homelanders?"

"Please, Charlie . . ."

"Who are they?" I shouted.

He glanced down again. I tried to hold him, but he was slipping away.

"Americans," he said. "Recruited by the Islamists. Because we're not foreigners. We don't draw suspicion. We can go places they can't go, do things they can't do. We're going to destroy this country from the inside . . . That's the plan. But you know this. You know all this. You're one of us. Please, Charlie."

"You're lying," I shouted down at him. "I love this country. I would never do anything to hurt it. You're a liar."

He slipped another inch in my grasp, another inch toward that fatal fall.

"Please!" he said.

I pulled him up. It took all my strength. Grunting with the effort, I stepped back from the railing, lifting him inch by inch until he could bring his own hand up and grab hold of the metal himself. Then I shifted my grip and helped him climb over. He tumbled, gasping, onto the bridge pavement. I bent over, hands on my knees, trying to catch my breath.

Orton lifted his hand. "The motorcade. They'll be here any minute. We've got to activate the bomb."

Rage erupted inside me. I reached down and grabbed the front of Orton's jacket. I dragged him off the pavement and brought his face close to mine.

"Listen to me," I said. "I don't care what you say. I don't care what you think. I'm not one of you. I'm not a Homelander. This bomb is not going off, you hear me? You're finished, Orton. I saw you kill those troopers and I'm turning you in."

He struck with lightning speed. His arm flashed across my wrists and hammered back at me, hitting me in the throat. I went down to the pavement, gagging. Through a blur of tears, I could see Orton staggering to the car. He went into the open trunk again. He worked at the mechanism.

I had to stop him. I looked around for help. The gun—his pistol—there it was, lying in the road about five yards away from me. Choking, I crawled toward it.

Orton stood up. He had a device in his hand—a small electronic box with a blinking red light on it. I knew what it was. He had finished activating the bomb and was ready to set it off by remote control.

I was almost at the gun. I was reaching for it. Crawling. I was just beginning to breathe again. I sounded like a creaking door as the air wheezed in and out of me. I reached the gun and wrapped my hand around its grip. I worked my finger into the trigger guard.

Orton spotted me. He walked quickly across the bridge. He kicked out and hit my wrist with the sharp tip of his shoe. The gun flew out of my grasp and went spinning across the bridge's surface.

Orton seemed about to go after the gun, but he looked over his shoulder and hesitated.

Then he took off in the opposite direction, running along the bridge.

Still wheezing, I worked my way to my knees and looked where Orton had looked. I saw the motorcade. It had just come into view around the corner. It was heading for the bridge. It would reach the entrance in sixty seconds, maybe less. Orton was trying to get off the bridge so he could blow it and send Yarrow and everyone with him to their deaths.

There was no chance for me to get to the motorcade, no chance anymore to warn them. By the time I reached them, they would already be on the bridge. I had to stop Orton. I had to get that remote.

Crying out with the effort, I got to my feet and raced after him.

He was nearly at the end of the bridge, but I was faster than he was. Even as worn out and battered as I was, the fear and desperation of the moment gave me the energy to race at top speed. I closed the gap quickly.

I glanced back over my shoulder. The motorcade was nearly at the bridge. I faced forward and saw that Orton had reached the bridge's far end. He turned, holding the remote, watching, waiting for the right moment to push the button. He saw me and cursed. I was going to reach him before the time was right.

He turned and tried to run farther, but he was too late. I threw myself at him.

I hit him low, around the legs. He toppled over and hit the road. The remote control was jarred out of his hand and skittered away from him.

I tried to climb over him, to get to it. Orton drove his elbow back and caught me in the side of the face. The blow knocked me off him. He pulled his way forward over the road and grabbed the remote again.

I looked back across the bridge. Yarrow's motorcade was just reaching the bridge entrance. There were only seconds left before he would be in the blast zone.

I looked back at Orton. He was getting a grip on the remote. He was turning to face the bridge, waiting for the cars to get out on it, over the canyon.

I lunged at him, grabbed the remote, and drove my palm down on the button.

"No!" Orton shouted.

The car in the middle of the bridge exploded. The blast was enormous, a billowing fireball that blotted out the sky. The force of it washed over me. The roar of it erased every other noise, every thought. And still, for another endless second, that orange ball of fire kept rising up and up, obscuring everything.

The bridge broke. The steel railings were torn apart like paper. Concrete poured down into the canyon below, the debris falling and falling endlessly before hitting the water and earth at the bottom with a noise washed away by the echoing blast.

I climbed slowly to my feet, staring at the devastation. For a long moment, I couldn't see anything beyond the explosion. The fireball was curling back into itself, but in its place was a rising column of black smoke that hid the far end of the bridge from view. It was another second or two before the breeze over the canyon blew the smoke aside and I could see what had happened.

The motorcade—it was still there. The cars had stopped well clear of the explosion. I had done it. Yarrow and his people were safe.

Orton saw it too. He was on his feet too. He let out a string of foul curses.

"Prince was right about you," he said. "He was right all along. After all our preparation. All our plans. You ruined everything."

Exhausted, I nodded. "Yeah," I said. "I guess I did."

"You rotten little . . ."

But suddenly his voice stopped. He stared at me with wide, frightened eyes. He looked down—we both looked down—and saw the bloody hole in the center of his shirt. He'd been shot.

"Oh . . ." He rolled his terrified eyes up to the sky. "Oh no."

Then he collapsed onto the pavement, dead.

I stared at him, uncomprehending. The rumble of the blast was still echoing and fading along the walls of the canyon.

Then it was gone, and a new noise surrounded me: the deadly rattle and whine of gunfire.

I lifted my eyes from Orton's body and looked back across the bridge. Secret Service agents and police had poured out of the cars of the motorcade. They were racing across the bridge toward where the bomb had blown a hole in it. Some had pistols in their hands. Some had rifles raised to their shoulders.

All of them were firing at me.

CHAPTER THIRTY-ONE

To Find the Truth

The whistling breath of the bullets whizzed past my ear. The dirt and rocks began spitting up on every side of me. I understood at once. They thought I was a terrorist, too, that I was with Orton. They thought we had tried to kill Secretary Yarrow but had made a mistake and set the bomb off too soon. Their bullets had caught Orton and killed him. Now they were trying for me.

I dove for cover. I was off the pavement in a second, working my way up the incline into the trees. I ducked behind a tree trunk for protection.

The lawmen on the far side of the bridge continued firing at me. Some of them were shouting now too. I could hear their voices but couldn't make out what they said. I didn't have to. I could pretty much guess. They were telling me to give myself up.

I didn't know what to do. I'd already been convicted of murder. Now they thought I was a terrorist too. How could I ever convince them that I'd blown up the bridge not to kill Yarrow but to save his life? How could I ever make them believe I wasn't one of the Homelanders?

I crouched there another moment in my confusion and my fear. The truth was: I didn't know what to believe myself. A court of law said I'd killed Alex Hauser. Orton said I was a Homelander just like him. I didn't remember anything after my ordinary life ended a year ago. Maybe it was all true. Maybe I was as bad as they said I was.

The shooting from across the bridge had stopped now, but the shouting continued. I could hear them more clearly: the voices telling me to surrender.

Then another voice came to me, a voice I remembered. That voice that whispered in my ear:

You're a better man than you know. Find Waterman.

Something deep inside me rose up to meet that voice. It wasn't just a vague hope. It was more than that. It was a powerful conviction of truth. I know it looked like all the facts were against me. I know the courts said I was a killer, and Orton said I was a terrorist. But I knew it wasn't so. I knew it to the bottom of my soul. I knew I'd never murder someone. I knew I'd never attack this country that I love. How could I turn myself in and let myself be put in prison before I had a chance to find out what had really happened?

I stayed there one last moment listening to the shouts from across the bridge. Then I stood up and began moving up the slope into the woods.

You're a better man than you know.

I didn't know what had happened to me this last year, but I knew my own heart. I knew who I was.

I still believe in you. I still love you.

And Beth too. I knew her. I trusted her. I knew she wouldn't have fallen in love with me if I were a killer.

Find Waterman.

I knew I was not alone. I was never alone. I knew that no matter how confusing things get, how many voices are shouting lies, how many wrong turns you take, how many dead ends you run into, there is always, always the truth to find, always the truth somewhere, burning, shining.

Never give in. Never, never, never.

I knew I had to find that truth no matter what.

I said a quick prayer as I worked my way deeper into the forest. Then I started running.

1. Charlie keeps a quote from Churchill in his wallet that inspires him and helps him focus. Are there words like that you go back to anytime you need encouragement or an extra boost of confidence? Do Churchill's words have the same effect on you that they do on Charlie?

2. After Charlie successfully finishes his demonstration at school, he stands on the stage and takes it all in. Do you have a moment like Charlie's, one that you

could call "one of the coolest moments of my life so far"?

3. One of the things that Charlie knows about himself is that he loves America and the freedoms we have here. Do you value those freedoms the way Charlie does? How does his patriotism make you feel?

4. Alex has had a difficult family life recently, but he also seems to be making some poor choices. Do you have any friends who have had changes in their lives and then started to seem like different people to you? Is there anything more that Charlie could have done to reach out to Alex? What have you done for your friends in those times?

5. Outside the jail, the person who releases Charlie's handcuffs tells him "You're a better man than you know." If you were in Charlie's shoes, what effect would those words have on you?

6. Even though Charlie doesn't remember the last year, he knows he cannot have done the things he is accused of because they are contrary to who he is.

What are some of the things that you believe that strongly about yourself? What would make you fight the way Charlie does?

7. Charlie faces incredible opposition in this novel. At which point were you the most afraid that he could not survive? Were there any places where you thought his adventures sounded like fun?

8. The last day that Charlie can remember was a really good day—his karate demonstration was a complete success and the number of the prettiest girl he knew was on his hand. If you had to pick a day in your life that would be the last one you could remember, which one would it be? What makes you want to hang on to that day?

9. *The Last Thing I Remember* closes with Charlie's resolve to find the truth, no matter what. If you were Charlie, what steps would you take to stay alive and find the truth?

Sometimes you have to go home
to find out who you really are

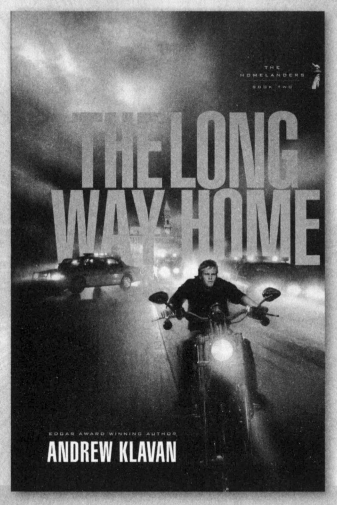

THE
HOMELANDERS

BOOK 2

THOMAS NELSON
Since 1798

You won't believe what comes next

THE HOMELANDERS
BOOK THREE

THE TRUTH OF THE MATTER

EDGAR AWARD WINNING AUTHOR

ANDREW KLAVAN

THE
HOMELANDERS

BOOK 3

THOMAS NELSON
Since 1798

Available November 2010

Q: Tell us a bit about The Homelander series and the direction it may be headed.

It's a story about a really good guy, a really upright, straight-arrow teenager, Charlie West, who goes to sleep one night and wakes up tied to a chair being tortured by terrorists. He has no idea how it happened or why or what they want. All he knows is he's got to escape. But when he does escape, he finds that it's not just the terrorists who are after him. He's wanted by the police as well. The series traces Charlie's efforts to stay alive long enough to find out what happened.

Q: What about Charlie West, the main character? Give us an idea of what he's looking for.

Well, he's looking for answers, first of all, but it's more than that. Everything in Charlie's life has been undermined and brought into question: his identity, his assumptions, his values. It's as if he has to reinvent himself, to start everything all over again. It sort of brings up some questions that I think are important for all of us to face: who are we and how do we know what's right and wrong? Are our values just an accident of culture or do they have some permanence?

What can we truly believe in and why? Charlie's got to figure all that out—and fast because if he makes one slip, trusts the wrong person, walks through the wrong door, the bad guys have got him and he's dead.

Q: At one point, one of Charlie's friends accuses him: "You walk around all sure of yourself. You think good is good and bad is bad. You think: work hard, pray to God, respect your parents, love America and everything'll be great." Is that really what Charlie believes?

No, of course not. He knows that everything isn't always great, no matter how hard you try to do what's right—in fact, no one knows that better than he does: I mean, he's a good guy and look what's happening to him! The whole world is trying to hunt him down and kill him. But Charlie does believe that there's such a thing as truth. Not just scientific truth, I mean, but inner truth, moral truth. And the question he now has to answer is: can he hold on to that kind of truth under fire, under duress? How can he keep his faith—*why* should he keep his faith?—when everything is so difficult for him? Charlie's life depends on him figuring out where good and evil lie and how to tell the difference.

Q: This is a novel that asks some big questions (about patriotism, faith, good vs. evil) through its fictionalized characters and storyline. What do you hope readers come away with?

Well, first and foremost, I just want readers to have the thrill of experiencing this story, of living with Charlie through this incredibly dangerous mystery. But the thing is, too, at moments of ultimate danger you frequently come face to face with ultimate truths. I mean, it's easy to sit in the safety of your room and think that good and evil don't exist or that faith doesn't really matter or that every problem can be solved by being "nice." But when you actually find yourself in a position where you have to fight with evil people or die, where you literally have only seconds to decide who to trust or who to do battle with—well, then those big issues suddenly become very real very fast. So I hope these are thrilling books but that the thrills are the kind that change your perspective a little.

Q: What does it mean to be patriotic in this day and age? Particularly for young Americans?

You know, it's become unfashionable to say so, but the simple truth is that America is unique. Unlike other countries, which were originally founded along racial lines, our country is founded on an idea—the idea of liberty that's enshrined in our Constitution. For Americans, patriotism doesn't mean nationalism or racial pride. It's not just love of this particular piece of earth either. For us, patriotism is primarily love and loyalty to this precious idea of liberty. The thing is, when you have a nation as powerful, well-protected, rich, and free as we've become, it's easy to think it'll always be that way. But in fact, even great nations can come under attack—from violent people and from misguided ideologies as well. In The Homelanders series, Charlie West has come face to face with some of those people—and some of those ideologies. And he not only has to pit his courage and his fighting skills against the bad guys, he also has to defend the American ideal against them with the understanding of his heart and mind.

Q: As a screenwriter, do you envision your fiction on the silver screen someday?

Well, look, it was a real thrill to see movies made out of my books. I mean, to have Clint Eastwood star in *True Crime*, Michael Douglas star in *Don't Say A Word*—how cool is that? But I've always been a book guy first and foremost. I love books and I love reading—so I don't really think about the movies when I write. Sometimes, when a book is finished, sure, I'll imagine about how it might look as a movie or which movie star might be in it. But while I'm actually writing the book, I never think about it at all. I try to pour all my energy into making the story and characters come alive on the page. Some day, a director and producer and screenwriter and actors may come together to produce their version of the story. But if you want to hear it first-hand, straight from the imagination that created the story, you have to read the book.